NIGHTLIGHT

$16.00

NIGHTLIGHT

A NOVEL

Michael Cadnum

St. Martin's Press

New York

Library of Congress Cataloging-in-Publication Data

Cadnum, Michael.
    Nightlight / Michael Cadnum.
       p. cm.
    ISBN 0-312-03897-6
    I. Title.
    PS3553.A314N54 1990
    813'.54—dc20   89-27053
                                                     CIP

First Edition
1 2 3 4 5 6 7 8 9 10

FOR SHERINA

*with special thanks to Adam and Jessica,
and to Craig and Joanne*

NIGHTLIGHT

1

The street outside had the sheen of pavement when it is just beginning to rain. Paul opened the notebook on the table and sat, but he could not read.

He had forced himself to get up because of the nightmare. He had been in a house, a house cluttered with books and clothes, as this apartment was cluttered. A comfortable place, homey. And just as he had felt contented he had felt, without any prompting from the dream itself, that this was going to be a nightmare.

He had tried to wake, but he was not able to, and as soon as he realized his failure someone was in the house. Someone fumbled through the kitchen, and into the hall, and Paul turned to run, but his legs were feeble. Too feeble to do more than twitch as the intruder felt down the hall, like a man without eyes, or even worse, like a man missing more than simply eyes. The intruder paused at the doorway to the room Paul was in, and Paul struggled to turn his head so he could at least see who it was, and he could not turn his head. He could not move at all, and the footsteps dragged across the floor, and a hand gripped his shoulder as he woke with a gasp.

Usually, he could not even remember his dreams. Now he was afraid to be alone. Paul prided himself on his level-headedness. Nothing made him nervous. He knew very well what was wrong with him, and it was very simple. He needed a vacation. Nothing elaborate. Just a break from this constant pressure to be fair and entertaining at the same time. He was sick of assistant managers calling them on the phone because the owner was too upset to talk.

He was sick of reading letters to the editors describing him as insensitive, ignorant, inept. Friends admired him, and envied his job. It was a dream job, one of them had said, helping himself to another chocolate truffle. The kind of job a person would do for free.

Paul used to think the same thing. It's amazing what a few years can do to a dream job. He listened to the patter of rain outside and debated whether to try to go to sleep again. It was three thirty, a hellish hour, the worst possible time to be awake. If he went back to sleep he would wake with a tender, swollen ache for more sleep. And if he stayed up he would spend the day feeling burned out.

He put his hand on the telephone but stopped himself. It was selfish to even think of calling Lise at this hour, although he wanted to talk to her very badly, desperately, as if she were the cure to all his problems. He took his hand off the phone as if it had suddenly grown painfully hot. He would call her later.

He got dressed and sat at the kitchen table, leafing through the pasted-up recipes he had invented, or guessed at from various sauces in some of the best restaurants in the world. His favorite recipes were surprisingly simple. The nutmeg fresh-ground over fettucini. The sprig of basil in the olive oil the sweetbreads had simmered in. The Scotch in the French-roast coffee, fresh-ground, with a pinch—no more—of sugar.

It was an eccentric collection of recipes. He thought of them as spare and elegant, Spartan and gourmet at the same time. He doubted the French chefs of the more highbrow restaurants would admire his chicken broth and chenin blanc veal, but it was exactly the sort of dish that tasted extravagant without incurring savage indigestion, the single most severe occupational hazard Paul suffered. True, French cooking was magnificent. He simply couldn't eat it every night and live.

For three hours he worked on his notes, sorting, recopying, until the phone rang, and he snatched it with pleasure.

"No, don't apologize. I'm sitting here, wide awake. I was going to call you."

"I had a terrible dream," she said.

"Me, too. I got up and was sitting here, wondering if I have a chance of putting together a cookbook."

"Why not? Everyone loves to cook."

"No, they don't. They hate to cook, except by rote or by imitation. Very few people are brilliant concocters of their own sauces. Which is what I mean by cooking. I don't mean simply preparing a dish. I mean 'cook' in the sense of 'compose.'"

"Snob."

"True. And I shouldn't talk. I tried to make mayonnaise once and came out with something that looked like gorilla semen. I'm just fed up with the entire subject of food. I wanted to be a sportswriter, you know. I wanted to get flown to Las Vegas to watch heavyweights hook each other bloody. Instead, I live like a spy."

She made a croon of sympathy and invited him to breakfast.

Paul crouched in his Volkswagen and shifted gears through the dark, wet streets of Berkeley, arriving at an apartment that was as cluttered and homey as his, although there were many more books. Books were jumbled everywhere he looked, and he had to lift a volume of the *Oxford English Dictionary* off a chair before he could sit. He used the magnifying glass to examine the hairs on the backs of his hand. His skin looked as vast and wrinkled as the hide of a woolly mammoth.

Lise nudged coffee from the bag into the electric coffee grinder. "I'm beginning to hate myself for doing my dissertation on Donne," she said. "Of course, when you spend a lot of time on a project you wind up hating it, no matter how you originally felt about it. The question is, do you want to end up hating something you used to love?"

His thumb was horrifying. The cuticle was ragged, and his thumbnail ridged, as glossy as a sheaf of balleen. He put down the magnifying glass. "Is it too late to change?"

She ignored his question. "I should have done Woolf. She's interesting, but doesn't give rise to any strong enthusiasm in me."

"What is it you are focusing on in Donne? Exactly?" Paul asked, feeling that he should know this already.

Her eyes narrowed. "Paradox."

"Ah."

"And I'm sick of it."

Paul had read only one or two poems by Donne in his entire life, and was slightly embarrassed at his ignorance. But he sympathized with Lise.

"Even when you love something you can get fed up with it," he said. "Maybe especially then, because you pay it so much attention."

She punched the button and the grinder chattered. She opened a filter and arranged it in the Melitta cone. He watched her with pleasure, admiring her lean sexuality, the early-morning frowsiness of her hair, the precise way she chose the cups and set them, handles just touching, beside the coffee grinder. One cup was beet-red, the other cloud-gray, both of them the products of local artisans. Paul thought them a little crude, but they would keep the heat of the coffee very well.

"I got Kona coffee," she said. "It was a little more—what's the matter?"

"Nothing. Well, actually, I don't like Kona. Too light. It has an odd nutty flavor, an aftertaste that is feeble, and it lacks body. A fault it has in common with Mexican Arabicas, although Kona is arguably better." He silenced himself. "I'm sorry, Lise. I've gone crazy."

"I don't mind. I'm not one of those idiotic women who identify with their ability to make coffee. I don't give a shit what you think of anything I make. You can fry your own eggs, too. This one here has a speck of blood in it. Means more hormones and better nutrition." Spots of red brightened her cheeks as she set a bowl before him. A raw egg stared up at him, red in the shape of a comma floating off-center in the yolk.

Paul looked up from the bowl. "I'm sorry, Lise. I really am."

"Maybe you've been doing it too long."

"I was just thinking that. I was thinking I need a break. Even a few days. I'm turning into the kind of person I always hated. Arrogant. Humorless. Impatient."

"It doesn't help to know that you're a lot smarter than most people," she said. "Damn near perfect. That most people are lucky to even be on the same planet as you are."

They had grown cheerful by the time she poured the coffee. She hesitated before giving him the cloud-gray cup. Outside, it was still dark. Drops elongated from the eave and broke free, silver spears

of water. He shivered, and cupped the coffee in his hands
thought you were a lot smarter than me. By a unanimou

She shrugged. "I don't know about that."

"You're the one getting a PhD in English. I squeezed out a BA in
journalism, and was lucky to get that. The food editor was in the
hospital with a burst appendix, and I lucked out with what everyone
swore was a plum."

She was plainly pleased with his high opinion of her, but she made
an expression of denial. She blew on her coffee, and he admired
the pucker of her lips. She looked better with no makeup. Smaller,
somehow, and passionate.

Breakfast, he thought, could wait.

He had to move books to make room in the bed, and books edged
into the side of his knee as he held her. They were quick, as if both
wanting to get somewhere they had looked forward to for years,
silent and working hard with their bodies. Her body surprised him
as always, so much more athletic than his, but making his body feel
powerful above hers, as she moaned and said his name in that way
that burned him.

Later, he scrambled the eggs, and when the toast popped up they
ate in silence. You couldn't surpass a scrambled egg, he thought.
You could enhance it, of course. A little parmesan and a sliced
mushroom or two, or fungi, as he liked to call them, with perhaps
some apricot chutney.

She was watching him. "Sun's coming up."

The window was the color of his cup. "A miserable day," he said.
"Although I actually like rain."

"It happens in November," she said idly. "This is when the rainy
season begins." She lay a hand on a book beside her plate. "I'd give
anything to take a break today."

"Join me tonight. I can always use help. No snide remarks about
being cheap. It's business, not pleasure. But—please come. I'd like
you to be there."

"So you won't be bored?"

"There are worse reasons."

"Shall I wear a disguise?"

"They don't know you that well. I, on the other hand, should probably wear a false beard. By the way, what was your dream about?"

She looked away. "It was just a dream. Except, it was the first nightmare I've had in a long time. It actually made me afraid to be alone. Isn't that silly?"

"What was it about?"

She shrugged, but he could tell that the dream had troubled her "It was just a nightmare. But if you insist . . ."

He made an expression of interest.

"I was in a house. A house I felt very comfortable in. And someone was suddenly in the house, and I couldn't wake up, and I couldn't move, and I couldn't even turn my head."

2

Mary Lewis waited in her garden. Only the roses still had flowers, and these were loose-petaled and huge, edged with brown. One or two were nearly perfect, though, she discovered as she felt among the thorns. The gardener did good work, and she must compliment him.

It had been raining, and it would rain again, soon. She crossed her arms, wishing for a sweater. And wishing for much more than that, she realized. Wishing that she could remake her entire life. Undo everything she had ever done. Why she had waited so long, she could not guess.

A sprinkler head oozed water. A finch paused on it, but fled immediately as Sandy stepped across the patio and announced the visitor, the guest, she supposed he was, but he was scarcely here on a social visit.

She was disappointed in the doctor. She had hoped they would send someone mature, robust and slightly gray, someone who looked wise.

"I hope you don't mind if we talk out here. I know it's cool, and I expect rain any minute. But I feel more at ease here."

"I don't mind at all," said the thin young doctor. "It's beautiful."

"Thank you. I don't think it's like any other garden in San Francisco. My father designed it. From the street, you aren't aware that it is here at all."

"You certainly aren't." The young man accepted coffee, and she repeated his name as if to test whether he responded to it. "Dr. Kirby?"

He said that, yes, he would like sugar, and used the silver tongs to select a cube.

"It's what you would call a hidden garden. You can't see it from the street, or from any of the surrounding houses. I think no one really knows it's here. It uses land that does not seem to be here at all."

She waited for him to respond, but he was hesitating over Sandy's petits fours.

"My father was fascinated by secret places," she continued. "I have often wondered if perhaps he had them build a secret room into this house. He could have, and no one would know it."

"Do you think he did?" asked Dr. Kirby, dabbing at his lips with linen that kept its folds even when shaken open, like the map of a totally empty countryside.

His interest was amusing, and made him seem, briefly, charming. "My late husband wondered. He even thumped walls and made measurements." Decrepit creature that he became, he had never been stupid. She collected herself. "He decided that every square inch of the house is present and accounted for. There is only this garden, this beautiful secret."

Dr. Kirby chewed, and sipped coffee.

"But you will wonder why I asked you here."

"Is there anything we can help you with, Mrs. Lewis?" asked the young man, setting aside his cup and saucer, adjusting the napkin beside him as if it hid a rabbit.

She could not begin to talk about it. After all these years of silence. It was simply too difficult. She could simply announce that she was going to give yet another grant to the hospital, so they could build a new wing for hydrotherapy, or plan a parking lot so their outpatients could park their BMWs closer to the magnolia trees.

But this was not why he was here. To plug the silence, she said, "I don't even know how to begin."

"Start anywhere you like. At the beginning."

She saw that he was used to people who had trouble talking. He was experienced in spite of his appearance, his off-the-rack polyblend, and his tattered knit tie. His eyes took her in, and she was pleased that she was looking especially good today. Her hair only slightly gray, and her figure still slim enough to draw attention, quite a bit of it. In her youth, she had been pretty without being beautiful. Now, on her best days, she was a little bit—dare she suggest it to herself?—beautiful. Classical, at least.

She studied her manicure. "Th' beginning."

He smiled helpfully.

"Do things have beginnings? Lives do, but lives are altered by things that happened long ago." She could continue in this vein for a long while. Dr. Kirby would never do anything but fidget. She could bore people, and waste their time, and they would resemble Egyptian masks of the dead, patient and cheerful, and interested in the void that surely—there was no doubt--was filled with promise, like passengers on a plane to Paris. She never bored people, except deliberately.

"We can choose to call a certain event a beginning," suggested Dr. Kirby.

"My family has always craved secrecy."

The roses across the lawn swayed in a brief gust.

"My father would be in pain," she continued, "and no one could tell. My mother kept her silence, no matter how she disapproved. And I carry on the tradition. Being a somewhat prominent family in society made us keep to ourselves. We hungered for a secret life. To avoid scandal, of course. But more than that. To have something no one knew about, something powerful because it was secret."

Dr. Kirby smiled, as if he knew all about secrets. An exterminator would smile in this way if told about roaches.

Under her beauty, if that's what it was, she was a sick woman. She knew it. She had enough sanity to admit that. She was not raving; she was not dangerous.

Except to one person.

"I am," she said, "very concerned about my son."

Sick. She should have gotten help long ago.

Dr. Kirby folded his hands. He seemed unwilling to interrupt her silence. "It's really too cold to be sitting out here," she said at last.

He did not move, but offered, "Shall we go inside?"

"No. Everything else in the house these days reminds me of my husband. He was"—she had never expressed it plainly before—"a drunk."

Dr. Kirby's pleasant face waited for her to continue.

"I married him because he reminded me of my father." That should tell him everything, she thought, but it won't.

"Your son," he suggested gently.

"Yes. My son." She watched a black bird listen for worms. How loud the surge of worm through soil must be to a bird. The bird stabbed, and came up empty. "To me this garden has always seemed like the center of the universe."

"It's very pretty." Said as if he did not really care for gardens.

"It's not pretty," she said. "Pretty is superficial. It's beautiful."

In which case, she realized, she herself could not really be beautiful.

"Did your son enjoy the garden?"

"He spent his entire life here."

He smiled blandly, not comprehending. Why hadn't they sent someone perceptive? Why did she have to spell everything out? She wanted someone who would see her, see this place, and immediately know her.

"I mean he lived here until he was an adult, and never left this house, this garden."

"Never?"

"Virtually." She said the word carefully, wishing she could wrap it around Dr. Kirby's neck. "I mean, and forgive me if I am vague, that this house and this hidden garden were his life."

He looked around at it through new eyes. He still did not seem concerned. He frowned, though, looking across at the pale roses, and touched the saucer beside him. "So that he never had much contact with the world outside?"

"The outside world," she corrected. "Because this is a world, too. A small world, but complete. In its way," she added.

"An inside world."

"Precisely."

"And you are telling me that your family had many inside worlds."

She was impressed. He was paying attention. She continued, "But I am not seeking help for myself."

"You are worried about your son."

"Yes, I am."

"Where is your son now?"

She whispered: "I don't know."

"You're no longer in contact with him?"

She blinked her eyes clear. "To put it very mildly."

"What makes you think something is wrong?"

She couldn't tell him about the dream. She couldn't tell him about the locked boxes. She couldn't tell him about the one other sort of help she knew well, the services of a locksmith.

She couldn't tell him how her father, dead for years, had seemed alive in this house, night after night.

She couldn't tell him the truth about Len.

3

When there is no light, the branches and the leaves of trees exude a light of their own. Through their skin. Through the membrane of nothingness that covers everything. Every twig. Every leaf.

But the best places were these, where the secret, buried people waited. Their long wait made a light breathe from the earth. The light filled the trees. My eye would not be able to see the light. But the light was there, and I would trap it, as hands trap the moth.

I climbed a wall, and balanced there, cradling the camera. I fell, and rolled, and now I was among the waiting strangers.

I had been hesitating to come here for years. But He kept calling. Come. Just for a visit. Take pictures of the place where I wait. My quiet kingdom. You know how much I love you.

Even now I trembled. I wept as I used to weep. Please, I used to pray. Please leave me alone.

But this was just a visit. See how the strangers lay in their great pleasure that I was among them now. My eyes could not see them where they rose from their secret places, and stood gazing at me.

Please leave me alone, I wept.

But they watched me. He has been waiting a long time, their silence said. See how He loves you.

My hands were trembling, but I clung to the camera, the thing I knew could see them. The lens was more subtle than the eye. I told myself: I'll take a few pictures, and then I can go. Just a few pictures.

That's right, He said, from His secret home, far across this field of stone monuments. This first visit you can take just a few pictures.

Seal them up in your camera, and take them home. We have time. I have waited so long for you to visit me.

Just a few pictures. Then I'll be done, I thought. I had always preferred this sort of light. I was winning prizes for the way I could make starlight look. But no one knew why I had been learning to coax light out of places where the eye could not see.

It was so I could crouch here, now, and aim the camera. Just three or four, and then I can go.

The camera was a solid mechanism. It made its pleasing click. It was my usual wide-angle lens, and it was capturing the place, and all its secrets, there was no question of that.

Come closer.

I crept across the cold grass, but then stopped myself. This was enough. I had done enough. It was only a visit. Now you will leave me alone.

I don't like us being apart like this, He said, that voice from the secret place. Come closer.

I closed my eyes. I did not move.

Please. Please leave me alone.

4

Paul clipped his pen into his pocket, and shrugged into the gray tweed jacket he knew made him look anonymous. Waiters like bland customers, and tend to make the sort of cheerful mistakes they avoid in the face of memorable diners. Drinks arrive that had not been ordered, the steak shows up done too well, or bleeding raw, if the waiter forgot you as soon as he saw your face.

His pants fit him well. He had not gained weight on this job, to his mild surprise. He had not developed an ulcer, either, which was more surprising. He ran a comb through his hair, and answered the phone absentmindedly, thinking it was the paper reminding him that they needed nine inches by tomorrow afternoon, one of those secretaries Ham hired and fired regularly, for mysterious reasons.

"Is this Paul Wright?"

He leaned against the wall. Someone about to beg to be reviewed, or, worse, to curse him for having said the worst possible things. He put professional distance into his voice. "Speaking."

"This is Mary. Your aunt."

He had mistaken the nervous, fluttery quality of the voice. He was delighted to hear from her. It had been so long since—and then he was quiet for a moment, remembering that it had been seven years since Uncle Phil's funeral. Time, he said brightly, had simply flapped its wings.

He was about to inquire how his cousin Len was doing, but her urgent voice interrupted him. "I need your help," she said.

"Of course," he said. "Anything I can do."

"I can't really tell you over the telephone," she said.

"I understand," said Paul, although he didn't. Anything could be said to anyone over the telephone. If the CIA wanted to be bored to death, that was its problem, Paul thought wryly.

She invited him to visit her the next afternoon, an invitation Paul accepted with pleasure. He had always liked Aunt Mary, but he had remembered her as less mysterious, a straightforward woman who never minced words. She was plainly disturbed about something, but controlled her voice carefully. She was not on the edge of tears. She was on the edge of something worse. Paul could not guess what. Not hysteria. Not worry. Something worse than worry.

She was afraid of something.

Lise swore as she dragged herself into the Volkswagen. "I got Parker Super Quink on my new wool skirt."

"It'll wash out," Paul said, knowing it was exactly the wrong thing to say.

She wanted commiseration, not advice. She folded her arms, and Paul fastened her seat belt for her, knowing the act would seem conciliatory. "I guess it will," she said at last.

"Tough day?"

"Little things kept going wrong. Broken pencils. Dropped cups. Two cups, not—thank God—my favorite red one, but that nice gray one, the one you used this morning. Smashed to powder when I ran hot water on it."

"Must have been a secret flaw."

"Yes. It made a pinging noise, like a string plucked. And it was all over the sink. I was so rattled I snapped another cup off at the handle." She laughed. "I had the handle in my fingers, but the cup itself waddled across the floor, slopping coffee all over."

The waiter sized them up immediately, and met the glance of the maitre d', who smiled them into a prime table, near a window, through which Paul watched geraniums shiver in the rain.

Standard East Bay Linen white table cloth, with a small, tufted hole near the tine of his salad fork. A fresh pink carnation in imitation Waterford. Wine list at only a forty-percent markup, the sign of a new restaurant begging business.

"They've made us," Paul said, flipping open the menu.

"How do you know?"

"Did you see the maitre d' touch the busboy on the shoulder when he spoke to him just now? When was the last time you saw a maitre d' touch a busboy? Panic has gripped the kitchen. It's like a submarine spurting water in there. The chef is putting on a show of courage. The assistant manager is phoning the manager who is due in in half an hour anyway. He'll call the owner. A command center is established by now. We'll get our ice water in seconds."

The busboy, in his white baggy sleeves, spilled a drop of water no bigger than a nickel. The young man held his breath, and, Paul imagined, calculated bus fare to Tijuana. The maitre d' strutted to greet two other customers, wearing a rictus of courtesy.

"The waiter usually identifies himself by name. 'Hi, I'm Al, your waitperson.' But he won't now, because he knows it makes me vomit. Or, so I've said. At this point, I've given up."

The waiter was smoother than the maitre d'. Crinkled his eyes and told them that the Soave was better than the Frascati. "It almost always is," Paul said when he had vanished. "You know what's grim for me is that it's like eating on a stage in front of dozens of unkind eyes. If I drop Gorgonzola on my tie, they'll put their heads together in the darkness and smirk. My father used to stuff the napkin in his T-shirt. Manners in my family was not sucking the goop out of the inside of our cream puff. This is a modest place. Middlebrow. In the loftier places I feel like a chimpanzee."

"You always act so suave."

"I wanted to interview Pete Rose. I dreamed of going to spring training and watching my boyhood heroes hit fungoes. A lot of kids hit imaginary home runs against the garage door. I used to keep score of imaginary baseball games. I like things to be commonsense and on paper. No guesswork. No opinions. Just events, recorded with an unbiased eye toward the truth. Christ, the waiter is consoling the maitre d'. They figure they've lost already. Maybe the chef has had a stroke. This is horrible. We should get up and leave."

The worst possible thing happened. The maitre d' approached them stiffly and showed his teeth, beginning the Speech of Greeting which always destroyed the last of Paul's appetite, through all its variations in all the various accents he had heard attempt it. The maitre d' extended the good wishes of the owner, and hoped that if anything were needed Mr. Wright would not hesitate to ask: It was the sole desire of the owner that they both enjoy this evening's meal.

Paul was relieved that no bribe of food or cash had been even hinted at. He responded that he was sure they would both enjoy their dinners, emphasizing the word *both*, so the staff might believe that an act of seduction was underway, not simply another column in the daily.

Paul ordered the *mista* of chicken livers and hearts, knowing that any restaurant with such an odd dish must be proud of it. He encouraged Lise to sample the veal, promising that if she didn't like it he would drop by Colonel Sanders' on the way home.

The dinner was excellent. Lise's veal was in a caper sauce, with a delightful flavor more intense than the usual lemon sauce that was so common. The capers were surprisingly attractive, friendly pealike shapes, but not as wrinkled as peas, and smaller. Paul's dish was delicious. It was hard to disguise the anatomy-lesson air of such a dish; he counted twelve hearts, and knew that they represented twelve separate lives. He acknowledged the presence of the livers, but it was the sauce that delighted him. It was a red wine sauce, and a demiglaze of beef had been added just before serving. He recognized the method as he tasted the first spoonful, and his admiration for the chef grew until he wanted to dash into the kitchen and shake his hand.

"Ordinarily," he said, "I visit a place two or three times before I review it, but I think I'll write this one up tonight."

"Maybe they knew you were coming."

"No one knew. Not even you. I am very careful not to mention any of my plans."

"Like a spy."

"Actually, this job is very much like being a spy. A detective, at least. I remember—or try to remember—to be fair, always. To weigh everything carefully. Not to trust other people's opinions. To ignore reputation and hearsay. To have no opinion until I have seen and tasted. What do you think of the wine?"

"It's having trouble standing up to all these flavors."

Paul was pleased that they shared the same opinion. "Exactly what

I think. Although I sometimes think that the Italian philosophy about wine with food is that it doesn't harmonize with the food so much as fit in with it. A chardonnay wants to bracket a food, wrap it in flavor, highs and lows, like a quartet. An Italian white, although thinnish by comparison, simply serves the food, on a plate, so to speak."

He nibbled at a pine nut tart, and tasted Lise's kiwi fruit tart, bypassing the mousse which he knew was made by a shop in Oakland that serviced six restaurants with excellent but indigestible chocolate desserts. The espresso was brought to the table in a stovetop espresso maker, a homey touch that didn't fit the pretensions of the restaurant, but Paul was expansive and forgiving and when the owner arrived, smoothing back his hair, gripping Paul's hand like an arm wrestler, Paul could tell him truthfully that his restaurant was a success.

The man nearly wept. "Was the veal to your satisfaction?"

"Quite."

"The *mista*? The salads?"

He had been given an order-by-order breakdown of the meal, no doubt wincing at little uncertainties. Paul reassured him. "Everything was excellent."

5

Aunt Mary lived in a handsome brick fortress in Pacific Heights. The mortar between bricks was a brilliant mossy green, and a cupid turned to one side on a small fountain to share a joke with someone invisible. Water danced above the simpering, muscular infant, joining the rain as it fell over the stout legs. Paul used his own fist, rather than the knocker, and hurt his knuckles.

Aunt Mary herself answered the door, although Paul had expected a tall, male servant. She squeezed his hand in greeting, and Paul realized how much he had always liked her.

He followed her into a library, a room he had not seen since his boyhood. Fire curled around a log the size of a man's torso in the fireplace, and the room was lined with what Paul supposed must be expensive books. Leather, some of it with a patina of age, some of it newish, and Paul could not guess where they still made books of that quality. Obviously chosen for their looks, rather than their contents, Paul guessed. His hand went out and selected a volume that looked especially weathered. It was in Latin, and the old pages turned with a crisp sound.

"P. Ovidii Nasonis," he read silently. "*Metamorphoseon.*" He closed the book as one closing the door to a temple. He turned and realized he had neglected his aunt, who waited patiently by the fire.

"I'm sorry. All these books—"

"You found the Ovid. It was one of your Uncle Phil's favorites. He translated parts of it, in an amateurish sort of way. He especially liked the part where Daphne turns into a laurel. He had a theory, and I agree with him, that transformations are inherently more fascinating to human beings than static entities. That we like dawn and sunset not simply because they are attractive to behold, but because they are thresholds."

Paul absorbed this, and accepted a glass of brandy. The liquor danced with the light from the fire, and Paul did not want to taste it, it was so beautiful. His aunt spoke about her late husband's love for books, his fondness for music, and Paul understood why he had seen so little of his aunt and uncle. Their lives had been complete, and Paul was not highbrow, or even interesting.

He thought this without malice. He was fond of his aunt, and enjoyed the sound of her voice. There was something in her tone, however, that told him that she was not at peace. There was something wrong, and he waited.

She stopped, abruptly, as if coming to the end of a chapter. When she began again her voice was deeper, softer but more intense. "I need your help, Paul. Phil would have been able to advise me, but I am alone now. It's a family matter—or at least I want it to remain that way. I have some modest standing socially, and I don't want a scandal. Don't misunderstand. I don't fear scandal, but I would rather avoid it."

Paul smiled, mystified.

"Len has disappeared." His aunt looked away, overcome for a moment. When she could speak her voice was even quieter. "He rented a little cottage up in the wine country somewhere. I don't know where, exactly. And I haven't heard from him for two months. He was always very good about phoning once a week; we have always been a very close family. I have made a few inquiries through friends, but no one has seen him. And I would very much appreciate it if you would . . ." Her voice faded. "Please go up and see if you can find him, Paul. I'm afraid something terrible has happened."

"Have you called the police? Or the sheriff? Whoever it is up there."

"Len is such a private person he would die if a sheriff poked his head into his studio. He would never forgive me. Besides, you know how newspapers are. One word of Len being missing and the *Chronicle* would have it on page one. Not that it's big news, but that's the *Chronicle*."

Neither of them had touched their drinks. Paul waited for something to be made clear. There was something peculiar in his aunt's tone, something she was not discussing.

"I will tell you why I am particularly disturbed. And why I don't want to have this talked about all over town. Len has always been interested in painting, and photography. He has always been a whimsical young man. Gifted, but a dreamer. And I have encouraged him. If you have a talent, develop it, I have always felt. But lately, in the last year or so, he has developed a new interest. He has developed an interest in what you would have to call spiritualism."

Paul's face betrayed confusion. She added, "Séances. Haunted houses. He became obsessed with the idea of attending meetings in supposedly haunted houses so he could photograph the ghosts. Well, it all sounds farfetched but harmless, but he carried it too far. He began spending nights in cemeteries. He showed me endless roles of film, special settings on the cameras to soak up as much light as possible. Naturally, some odd things showed up on the film."

"What sorts of things?"

"Blurs. Nothing. Just things that you had trouble making sense of." Her voice was sharp for a moment. "Len thought that every time he picked up a stray cat on his film he was seeing a spirit."

She sipped her brandy. "He finally found a place up north somewhere he said was a legitimate 'place of haunting.' That's what he called them. Not 'haunted houses.' So he left to inhabit this 'place of haunting,' some two months ago. And I have not heard from him since. Of course, he may have sprained an ankle, I tell myself. I should call the sheriff, but I know that he is probably up there with his camera and sound equipment and would be furious with me if some yahoo deputy came clumping along. Len is a very intense person, and I have to respect him, but I can't sit still any longer."

"So you want me to drive up there, tell him to call home, and leave it at that."

She relaxed. "That's exactly right. That's all I want. Drive up, and drive back. The only catch is—I don't know exactly where the cottage is. So it might be difficult for you to find it. Time-consuming. And so I want to compensate you for your trouble—"

"Absolutely not. I will not hear of it. I was very much in need of a vacation. This is exactly the sort of break I need. Besides, I always liked Len. I haven't seen him for years, but he was always such a talented guy. Always drawing and taking pictures. We used to play with his train set. I was always proud to have such a smart cousin."

"I can give you a key to his studio here in the city. It's in a warehouse off First Street. A cavernous place; I only saw it once. Perhaps he has an address or something there, some way of knowing where the place was and . . ."

Paul pulled at his lower lip. "You want me to check up on him."

"Please."

Paul stood and wandered to the window. "Maybe you need a detective."

"If you don't want to do it, Paul, I understand." She added, "I've had some experience with detectives."

Her voice had become dry. She turned away from Paul and watched the fire. "Your Uncle Phil had an affair at one point during our marriage. I contacted a detective to find out who was involved. It was an established firm, a distinguished-looking man. When it was all over, I felt entirely sleazy. Phil confessed all of a sudden one night, but didn't name the woman involved. The detective arrived the next day, with telephotos of my best friend on a beach at Lake Tahoe. I was appalled, of course, but the worst thing was the pornographic glitter in the detective's eye. This is, as I said, a family matter."

"I understand."

"I have an envelope with directions to his studio, the studio key, a letter giving you permission to act on my behalf, and some cash against expenses which I ask you to accept, with my gratitude."

"You knew I would agree to do this."

"I hoped you would. And I read your reviews. They are the reviews of a curious man, who likes to taste new things. A man who prides himself on his common sense. On his ability to notice details. A man who is impatient with his own ignorance."

Paul blushed, flattered, but also amazed that she could have touched his vanity so well.

"By now you, too, want to find Len. Your curiosity is aroused."

She either guessed well, or she knew Paul's nature. Paul agreed that she was right. His curiosity was very much aroused.

Paul paused before a small painting on the wall. A man, evidently a shepherd, looked up from his seat at the foot of a tree. An angel addressed him, a diaphanous figure the size of a large rabbit. The angel was painted in white, with quick strokes of the brush. In the distance was a city, walls and towers displayed awkwardly, in a perspective that struck Paul as crude. The horizon beyond was lost in blue, and the entire painting was discolored, whites gone yellow, blues going gradually gray.

"A Patinir. Joachim Patinir died in 1524. Flemish, of course, and arguably the first Western artist to specialize in landscapes. What you see here is a shepherd awakened by an angel, perhaps the angel of death, but here the experts differ. Death is usually depicted as a virtual caricature. A dancing, grinning skeleton. So perhaps this is simply an angel." His aunt stood close to the painting, as if she had never seen it before. "As if in those days they expected angels to show up before shepherds, like a swarm of gnats."

"He looks surprised," offered Paul. "As if he were not aware of the custom."

She did not answer at once. "At any rate," she said, shaking off a thought, "I don't believe it is the angel of death. Some other heavenly messenger, with some other tidings. Certainly there must be good apparitions as well as evil ones."

"This is beyond my field of expertise," Paul said, tugging his nose. "I don't believe in any sort of spirit."

"You wouldn't," said Aunt Mary.

"Everything will be fine," Paul said.

"I don't expect instant results," she said, in a way that seemed a rebuff. "I am very patient. Take your time, but please begin soon."

A bad thought touched Paul. "Is there something you're holding back? Something I should know?"

"Nothing. Except a feeling I have—a hunch. A feeling that Len is in a strange kind of trouble. And that it has to do with his research."

"You mean, his ghost hunting."

"Thank God for your common sense," she said. "But Len takes it very seriously, and Len is not stupid."

"Everything will be fine," he repeated.

"I hope so. I wake at night sometimes, and I am afraid to be alone. I, of all people. I have always been a rock. A sensible person. So steady. Even during my husband's infidelity I waited, always sure of myself, never panicking. But lately, I've had the most terrible dreams. They seem so real."

She opened a door that swung too silently. Their footsteps made no sound across the carpet. A desk drawer opened with a sound like a cough. She pressed the envelope into his hand. She turned away, as if she did not like to see the envelope, or to be reminded of what it contained.

Paul wanted to leave then; he did not want to stay in this house. It was too cold, and too empty.

"Always the same dream," she continued. "I am in a house, alone. And then there is a sound, and someone is in the house, in a distant room. And they begin fumbling through the house, as I try to move, and I can't. I am utterly incapable of movement, of even turning my head, as if a powerful force held my skull in its grip."

Paul paused in the garden, and watched the water of the fountain mingle with the rain as it sprinkled the cupid. The cherub looked to one side, with a grin. His cheeks were fat, and fatter with the effort of a grin that could be called lewd. The eyes of the boy angel had no pupils, but he seemed to be looking at someone only he could see, someone who provided the obscene joke that the angel enjoyed. His wings sprouted from his shoulders, and from the top of his spine sprang a rigid black tube. Water jetted from this black pipe and fell back on itself, with a sound very much unlike rain. A patter of water, but deliberate, artificial, the sound of someone pretending to laugh.

"Paul." Aunt Mary's voice stopped him. She held on to the front door, and did not speak for a moment. "I don't think there's a phone at the cabin."

Paul waited, the chatter of the water the only sound.

"I want you to call me within the next three days, whether you've found him or not."

Paul shrugged. "Sure. No problem."

He wanted to sound calm and responsible, but all he could think was: the dream.

She has the dream.

6

For some reason crazy people and derelicts tended to spend working hours on the steps into the building, and Paul, for some reason, always said good morning to them. He had even become familiar with a savage-looking man with huge yellow teeth who nodded not his head but his entire upper body in greeting and said, "How you doin'," in response.

Paul never knew whether or not this was a question that required an answer, but on this morning he responded, "Very well, thanks," and the man shrank back into the shelter of the eaves, beside the newspaper vending machine chained to a pole.

Paul shook himself out of his rain coat, but did not bother to hang it anywhere. "Gotta see the Ham," he told the secretary he had never seen before.

"Yeah, Paul," said Hamilton, mussing up his gray hair as a way of greeting.

Paul stood still in the center of the room, meaning that he would take more than three seconds, and that he needed to sit somewhere.

"Move some of that shit," Hamilton said, waving a hand. A cigarette scribbled smoke into the air. "Berkeley High is having a field trip upstairs, and we all had to loan chairs."

Paul dropped three phone books to the floor, and set a clipboard of blank yellow paper carefully on top of them. He sat, and said quickly, as he had planned for hours, "I need some time off."

Ham put his feet up and scrunched his features with one hand. His face momentarily assumed new creases, then fell back into its usual folds. He blinked to focus his eyes, and leaned forward on his elbows. This was all a way of demanding an explanation.

Paul kept his silence.

Ham cleared his throat. "Time off."

People on the *Gazette* liked to quote small portions of previous statements as a way of negating them. It was a habit Paul found delightful, except when it was used against him. "Off," Paul said.

"Why?"

"Family emergency."

"Oh, for Christ's sake. What the hell's a family emergency? And while you're thinking, get up and shut the door, because I don't want to embarrass you before the secretary."

"Secretary? You mean your latest hobby horse out there?" Paul shut the door, but slowly.

"Do you have a review for us?"

Paul pressed his heart, and paper crackled.

"You've been borderline late three weeks running."

"Borderline, though, right?"

"Don't give me any of your horseshit, Paul, because I'm tired, the paper is broke, and you are very lucky to have a job. It's the easiest newspaper job in the state. You file nine little inches, twenty-three centimeters, a week, and clip out some recipes you steal from *Family Circle* every Saturday, and that's it."

"It's destroying my personality," Paul said calmly.

"Personality."

Paul let his features assume the expression of a Buddha.

"I could name a hundred people who would kill to have your job."

Paul shrugged so hugely his neck creaked. "This is all beside the point. There is an emergency in my family."

Ham studied Paul's right eyelid. "What?"

"My cousin has disappeared." As soon as he spoke, he knew it was a mistake. His first, but he could not afford many.

"Your cousin," Ham said slowly.

That had been the weak part. The disappeared part had been solid. "He has vanished."

"Life is hard."

"So I may skip a column or two."

"Write them ahead."

"I can't."

"Why not?"

"Because I'm sick of it. I'm sick of eating béarnaise and snails and that incredible style of food where they put a piece of lox next to a pickled brussels sprout and call it a salad."

"You've never eaten béarnaise and snails."

"I didn't mean together."

"You're lazy," said Ham, squashing out his cigarette.

Paul rolled his eyes, but he knew he was winning. Ham was already pinching another filterless out of the pack, and leaning back in the chair. A lecture was about to begin, and a lecture was the tax paid on a liberty.

"Lazy," Ham continued. "I make you a celebrity. And what are you? Not even thirty. When I picked you, you couldn't tell a bagel from a—one of those little inner tubes people who have had hemorrhoid operations sit on."

The image made both of them thoughtful.

Paul was thirty-two, a fact which seemed like something that could be used against Ham in some way. He could not think of a way. He tugged the review from his jacket. He offered it to Ham.

"New Sicily." Ham glanced at Paul and looked back at the review. "What is it with you and Italian food. You don't like Chinese?"

"Sure," Paul said, feeling that it would have been better to say nothing. Ham was going to destroy this review, tear it up, and say that Paul had to have another review in half an hour. Paul would threaten to quit. Ham would tell him to leave. When they met again, they would be calm.

It was true that Paul had become something of a celebrity. A year before the newspaper had run ads featuring Paul's smiling face. The campaign flattered Paul, in a mild way, until he began seeing his face on the sides of AC Transit buses everytime he went for a walk. He had become reluctant to be on the same street as a bus.

The trouble with Ham was that Paul actually liked him. He had all the charm of a very old and very fierce reptile, but Paul admired him. Ham knew what he was doing. He was intelligent, and he believed in doing a job well.

Ham's scowl was still in place, but there was the slightest twinkle in his eye.

"You younger guys. You expect a lot of things from life that isn't going to happen. You draw cartoons for a few years, and you figure—I'm pooped. I need a break. You have a prize job, a job I would personally bleed for, and you piss and moan like you were covering the Donner party. Where is your desire to work? Where's your hunger to work, until you can't see straight, and to keep on going, because you have this need to keep going, this need to make something of yourself? To prove something."

Ham smoked, reading the review. "I was sportswriter here for years. I won't tell you horror stories about living on coffee and Camels for weeks at a time. Sometimes, it was fun. Sometimes working at the city dump is fun. I sat at ringside dozens of times. And got sprinkled with blood. My cuffs stained with it."

He tossed the review to Paul's side of the desk. "It's a good review. Take it to Luke."

It was a dismissal, and Paul had succeeded. He felt triumphant, but did not feel like celebrating. He handed the review to Luke Hand, the features editor, without speaking. Luke lifted an eyebrow to say that he saw it, leave it there.

Ham passed him, and paused at the men's room door. "Take care of yourself," he called after Paul, the sort of casual farewell Paul had heard uttered a thousand times.

Except this time he kept repeating it, all the way down the steps. Take care of yourself.

7

They each packed a small, nearly identical suitcase. "Matching ugly luggage," said Lise, tossing her suitcase next to his.

She was very excited, and of course she wanted to go; it would be an adventure, she said. Paul was delighted. It was their first chance to spend time together away from the clutter of their separate lives.

She pelted him with questions as they drove across the Bay Bridge. "He was an interesting guy. A few years younger than me, always had a camera around his neck. The kind of kid who had a telescope and a microscope, a scientific person, but only in that he was very interested in looking at things. He had an expensive HO-scale train set. We used to cause train wrecks, on a miniature scale. I've always liked people who seem smart."

"Was he . . . too smart?"

"Not really. Just very curious."

"What's the big mystery?"

"He vanished."

"But, what else?"

Paul had been embarrassed to mention ghost hunting. It made his cousin sound like a fool. He told her, briefly, about the attempts to photograph ghosts, and the supposedly haunted house, making an expression of mild distaste. "He was a very likable guy. Very curious. It was probably just a passing hobby. The way someone else might take up birdwatching for a while. I always liked Len a lot. I'm sure this is one of the unspoken reasons for my aunt asking me to look for him."

A gust pushed the Volkswagen into the next lane. Paul struggled with the car. "These damn Bugs blow all over the place," he said. "My secret theory, and I think my aunt was thinking along the same lines, is that Len has a homosexual lover somewhere up in the wine country, and has become hopelessly involved with him. I mean, it happens. This is why she doesn't want even the slightest chance of publicity. All of this ghost business is irrelevant, just the pastime of a man who doesn't have to work for a living. Maybe little more than an excuse for unexplained absences."

"But how exciting!"

"A homosexual?"

"No, a haunted house! It's fascinating!"

Paul made a world-weary smile. "We'll have fun."

"I wrote a paper on the etymology of the word *ghost* just last year. The word has a very interesting history. Its origin is, to make a long story short, mysterious. That's why I wrote about it. I thought I could clarify the mystery."

"Did you succeed?"

"Not at all. It comes from a pre-Teutonic word meaning 'fury.' It's related to the Old Icelandic 'to rage.' Whatever the difference between 'rage' and 'fury,' it amounts to the same thing: Ghosts are trouble. It's as if at some time in the distant past everyone understood that ghosts are dangerous."

"So that to ancient superstitions, ghosts were always angry."

"Not angry. Furious. There's a lot of difference between anger and rage."

They found the warehouse on a side street cluttered with wet trash. A stringy dog stopped and sniffed in their direction, then skulked up the street. Paul nearly slipped on the cracked sidewalk, but they both trotted through the rain, and up the steps. "He was always a fairly organized person," Paul said, finding the key in the envelope. "I'm hoping that we can make sense of his files."

"You know that what we are doing is not quite right."

Paul looked up with mock surprise.

"Sneaking into someone's privacy like this. What if he's in there now? What will we say?"

"Hello, Len. He'd be glad to see us."

"Would he be glad to know that we had a key?"

"Maybe *glad* is too strong a word. He wouldn't mind as much as some people. Of course, I haven't actually seen Len in years. Maybe he's changed."

The stairway was dark. The wooden steps were dusty, and the dust stuck to the soles of their shoes. They climbed toward the bright expanse of the studio above them, and emerged into it. A bank of windows let the gray-bright day illuminate the warehouse. The roof was high above them, a tangle of girders. The vast floor was bare, the entire place vacant, except for a crowd of furniture in one corner.

"You could play football in here," Paul whispered.

"It's huge!"

They reached the furniture, and ran fingers over a dusty desk. A draftsman's table was equally dusty; every object had not been touched for a long time. It was a normal-size office and bedroom dwarfed by the immensity of the building. There was even a television. A closet had been built of unfinished plywood. It was stamped "exterior grade," and the door was open a crack. Paul peered inside.

"Darkroom," he said. "No files, though."

"He doesn't keep files. He has a computer." Lise leaned over a small, blank screen. She pushed a switch and it squeaked. A green dot flickered and stayed on in the upper left corner. "Everything he wants to keep is stored here."

"He was organized."

"You gave me the impression he was a whimsical fellow."

"Well, he was."

"This is the working place of a very organized person. Look," she said, whisking aside a shower curtain. "A toilet. A sink." She touched an empty toothbrush holder attached to the wall. "He's much tidier than most men."

"You're good at this. What we are looking for is an address book. Somewhere he might have put the address of the place he was going to visit." The pad beside the phone was blank. A single, well-sharpened pencil leaned against the coils of the phone cord like a miniature javelin.

"I don't want to look through his dresser," said Lise.

Paul tugged open the top drawer and saw a pile of jockey shorts. It was a neat pile, and beside it was a single white athletic sock, folded neatly. He closed the drawer. "He's taken all his socks. All the ones with mates, anyway." He glanced into the other drawers, but he saw only clothing, or places where clothing had been.

The place was tidy and benign. There was a lack of the odds and ends Paul expected to find, and which a person would find in Paul's own apartment. Scraps of paper, random paper clips, half-read books, magazines, empty cups. Perhaps when he left this place he had cleaned it compulsively, as people will before leaving on a journey.

"I get the feeling he wasn't expecting to come back here for a while," Paul said, touching the cold surface of a hot plate.

"There are hardly any books."

"I don't think Len was much of a reader. Here's an old *Webster's,* and one of those godawful *Good Housekeeping* cookbooks. If he had a working library, about photography and such, he took it with him." He ran a hand along the spine of a three-ring notebook, the sort of blue canvas binder a student might use. He slipped it off the shelf.

Lise plucked something off the bulletin board. It dangled a white tag, which she peered at, and then she said, "Look!"

The tag read, *Dup.*

Paul fished into his pocket and brought out the key to the warehouse. It matched one of the keys. The other, a bronze brown key labeled *Schlage,* was enigmatic. "If this is a dupe, too, what's it a duplicate of?" he wondered.

"Nothing interesting, I'm afraid," she said. "Why would he leave a spare key to a place he was going to visit lying around? Why would he even have a spare key? Anyway, this isn't a house key."

Paul fingered the slim length of metal. "You're right. You really are good at this. This is more like a key to an attaché case, or a desk. Or"—and he put out his hand to touch a green metal box which was not locked—"one of these metal boxes you usually don't even bother to lock."

"What's in it?"

"The sort of stuff you might think about locking up, but would usually forget to." He held up a handful of bank statements, and envelopes of canceled checks, all fastened with pink rubber bands.

Lise snapped a rubber band off an envelope fat with checks. She sorted her way through there, lips pursed. Paul turned his attention to the blue canvas notebook. He opened it, and it made a crinkling sound, like something new that had not been used much.

The notebook was filled with stiff plastic pages, and photographs had been fitted into slots in the plastic. A white label was pressed neatly into place beneath each picture, and careful handwriting, like the handwriting of a draftsman, deliberate, quick printing, described each picture. *Colma 3-18, 2:15,* read one caption. Above it was a picture of a dark green smear. Many captions, many dark pictures, deep shades of blue and green.

When he realized what he was looking at, he closed the notebook.

"What's the matter?" asked Lise, looking up from a handful of checks.

"I'm beginning to think that Len was very strange indeed. I'm looking through a photograph album he rigged up. Thinking I might see some naked women. Or birds, anyway. Sunsets. Instead, look."

"What are they?"

"Photographs of cemeteries. Look, you can see the nameplates in the grass. Headstones over there. He went to the cemetery many times. Look, over a period of weeks. They aren't very artful, either. I mean, they're boring. They don't show a damn thing. Like he was deliberately taking the dullest pictures he could."

"Or like he wasn't interested in showing the usual things. Moonlight through the headstones, things like that."

"Long stretches of lawn. Actually, very nice, when you figure that the available light was lousy. That's why I couldn't figure out what I was looking at first. Patches of grass taken at three in the morning."

"He was trying to take pictures of spirits," she said.

"Yes. I knew that already. And now I see it. The man is crazy."

"This isn't the studio of a deranged person."

"I don't mean that he is mentally ill. I just mean, he has a very weird hobby."

She leafed through the album. "I wonder what he was looking for. If you saw a ghost, what would it look like?"

Paul turned away from the pages of the album, unable to think of anything but the dream. The steps in the hall. The hand on the shoulder.

"Crazy," Paul breathed. "A fool's errand."

"I don't see anything that looks like a ghost," Lise said, sounding disappointed.

"What would a ghost look like? Stupid question, or little more than theoretical. But you could be looking right at a ghost in any of those pictures and not know it." Paul stopped himself, suddenly irritated with this huge room. He got up and pushed a button on the computer. The machine sighed, and the dot vanished from the corner of the screen.

He laughed. "I can't get over the fact that a grown man would spend all this time and effort chasing ghosts. What a waste."

"You don't believe in ghosts," she said, closing the notebook. It was a statement, not a question.

"No." He did not ask if she did.

She slipped the notebook back into its place on the shelf. "Maybe he doesn't either. Maybe he is out to prove that there are no ghosts."

"Maybe," he said, doubtfully. "But it's impossible to prove a negative proposition. We can't prove that his address is not in this room. If we can't find it, all it means is that we can't find it."

"We don't have to find it," she said, holding up a check.

Paul held out his hand, but she was coy. "'North Coast Realty.' On the bottom it says, 'Deposit, Parker Cabin.'"

Paul held the check to the light from the windows high above, as if he could see through it. He turned it over. Pink bank stamps, and a line of fine ink, as if one of the check processing machines had leaked slightly. It was his cousin's handwriting. Instead of delight at the discovery, he felt sorry to see his cousin's handsome printing, his well-formed signature.

His sorrow confused him. Didn't he want to find his cousin?

"The phone is dead," she said. "We'll call on the way."

"You like this, don't you?"

"Of course I do. It's an adventure."

8

———

Paul did not speak all the way down Market Street. When they were on the freeway, he said, "I don't know why we want to go looking for such a fool."

She studied him. "What's the matter?"

"Nothing. Really, nothing. I just can't believe that a grown man would be so wrapped up in ghost chasing that he would spend night after night taking pictures of nothing."

"I don't believe in them." She said it as if to prove a point. "But I have a sense of humor about it. It's fun to imagine that there are ghosts, for a moment. To entertain the fantasy. It doesn't hurt."

He shrugged. Maybe, he thought. He could not explain why such a foul mood had suddenly gripped him. Something about the check. No, that wasn't it. Something about the pictures in the album. The dark expanse of blue-green lawns.

He found himself glad that they had left the album exactly where they had found it. As if it had been a disgusting thing, filthy and sickening to look at.

"So what, if your cousin liked to take pictures of nothing?"

"I don't like to see intelligent people waste their time," he snapped.

She ran her fingers through her hair, acting indifferent, but Paul could tell that she was surprised at his sudden anger.

"I just don't like to see it," he repeated lamely.

He was lying to himself. The thing that bothered him was that, looking back in his mind, he realized that the pictures hadn't been completely empty. There had been glints off to one side in one picture, higher in another, streaks of light the eye mistook automatically as flaws in the print, and dismissed without examination, the way the eye ignores the speckles in a bad print at a bargain matinee.

There had been things in those photographs that hadn't belonged there.

"I'm sorry," he said. "I don't know what's wrong. It only proves how badly I need to get away from everything."

"People need to believe in things like ghosts, sometimes," Lise said, filing her thumbnail. "Our age is so matter-of-fact. We don't believe in life after death. We don't believe in any world but this one. This prosaic, empty landscape."

Paul glanced out the side window, through the steam on the glass. The Napa River emptied into the bay, shining, canvas-gray water spreading into broader, grayer water. The landscape was empty, he agreed to himself. He liked it empty.

But he wanted to be careful to agree with Lise, and listen to her, and show her the best aspects of himself, because he had plans for this trip. Plans that did not include the mere search for a wayward cousin. Ordinarily, he would not be the least nervous about such a plan. But he found it amusing that he was.

At some point during the next few days, he planned to ask Lise to marry him. He was a sophisticated man, and charming, and of course she would accept. They had known each other for three years, and she was probably wondering why he hadn't asked long before. Paul gripped the steering wheel a little more tightly. He had his reasons, he thought. Until recently he had considered himself the sort of man who would never marry. There had been a wild affair ten years before, a passionate, sweaty fling with a beautiful landlady that had made him think of marriage, except that she had been entangled in a divorce that promised to drag on for months.

He had nearly asked the landlady, though. He had rehearsed the question at night, alone in his own room, still aching from his visit to her, aware of her two flights down, asleep, breathing fumé blanc into her tastefully decorated chamber.

And then, like one of those maple sugar candies in the shape of a deer or a woodsman, which pause on the tongue and then vanish, painfully sweet, the beautiful landlady decided that the divorce was not to be, and a handsome—heavyset, but handsome—spouse returned, grimly sure of himself. And husbandly, too, a quality Paul did not have, and did not think he could ever have, the ability to please a woman over the long run.

Thank God he had never asked her, Paul thought, rolling down the car window just a crack to help clear the windshield. His defeat was secret, not a defeat at all. The potential wife faded into simply a more-passionate-than-normal escapade. But he had learned a lesson. He had told himself never again, ever, to consider marriage. But it was not the considering that was the problem. It was the asking and being refused. The asking and finding out that there was a distant lover who was coming back, after all, and here he is now on the doorstep, box of mixed chews under his hairy arm.

Not that Lise had a lover tucked away somewhere. He didn't think so, anyway. But marriage might be against some principle in her, some man-eating shark that sulked inside her like a call to the cloth. She might have a horror of marriage. And, perhaps, a secret horror of Paul which his proposal might bring out.

These were considerations that were probably not worth thinking about for even a moment. But he couldn't help it. He lacked, in spite of his self-assurance as a critic, a final touch of confidence. As if his strength as a journalist had to be offset with a growing uncertainty regarding women.

Life is complicated, Paul consoled himself, as if an obscure truth was a salve. "Life is complicated," he sighed aloud.

"Yes," she agreed.

"You never know," he added, in an attempt to disguise the fact that he had been thinking aloud.

"No," she said sadly. "If we knew, it would make a great deal of difference, wouldn't it?"

"Of course," he said, mystified.

"Would you take more risks if there were?"

"Were what?"

"Life after death."

"Risks?" he asked thoughtfully. "No, of course not."

"I would."

"Why? Do you go around ruining good clothes just because you know there are other clothes in the world, that are just as nice, maybe even better? We naturally want to conserve the life we have. Naturally." The word seemed weak, so he repeated it. "Naturally," and then he turned into a gas station to ask directions.

No one emerged from the gas station office, so Paul climbed out of the car and ran, hunched against the rain. There was no one in the office. A voice called, "Right there."

A boy with greasy hands stood in the doorway, holding forth his hands to show why he had not responded sooner. His fingers were black, shiny black, and a drool of the stuff wended slowly down his arm. "Fill it?"

"No, I just need to find North Coast Realty. It's on L Street."

"No problem." They both walked to the wall, where a map of Saint Helena was thumbtacked. "You're here. You want to go here." A forefinger left a dim black kiss at the edge of town. "They might not be there, though."

"I called ahead," Paul said.

But the boy had left him, and Paul was reluctant to step forth into the rain. It was already late afternoon, or perhaps not so late. The gray sky made it dark. The clock above the map said it was nine on the nose, and Paul wondered if it had died at exactly that moment, or if someone had moved the hands to that position.

"No problem," he said, wiping the inside of the windshield with a Kleenex.

"Turn on the heater," she said.

"It doesn't work very well. It never did." This was a cheerless thing to say, and it made him sound incompetent. He turned the dial to High.

North Coast Realty was a log cabin painted red. A redwood tree towered over it, and Paul paused under the tree to comb his hair, before jogging to the door and finding it locked.

He swore and knocked. There was dim movement somewhere inside, and the knob twisted like an object trying to escape. The door opened, and a huge pale face smiled down upon Paul.

The man seemed delighted, and kept Paul's hand a moment longer than normal. "Ed Garfield. And you are"—he touched his ear lobe as if it were the seat of memory—"Paul Wright. The restaurant fellow."

Paul agreed brightly that he was indeed.

"So how can we help you?" The man had a comfortable voice, strangely like a man pretending to be a talking cartoon creature, a friendly bear, or a wise old horse.

Paul had explained on the telephone, but perhaps the man wanted to hear it in person. The man folded large wrinkled hands over a woolly sweater, and leaned back in his chair.

Paul finished.

The man looked up at the ceiling. "I remember the young man perfectly well. I only do a little managing nowadays. Semiretired. Wife not well . . ."

Paul made a murmur of sympathy.

". . . and I don't know. I could always take work or leave it alone."

They both laughed about leaving work alone.

"But you know. I really can't help you."

Paul straightened in his chair.

"Can't. Your young man said not to let anybody bother him in any way. Not a soul. For any reason at all. Period."

The man—it was hard to call him something so blunt as "Ed"— said these words in the voice of a Walt Disney character. But his eyes were the twinkleless organs of a man who had handled a good deal of money in his day, and could sell anything to anybody.

Paul appreciated this sort of man. This baggy-faced oaf would never go into the restaurant business, a business prickly with so many risks. He would stay forever in real estate, his investments greening under the steady rain.

Paul relaxed. "You're right, of course. I would do exactly what you are doing."

"Of course, in the emergency situation. A mother. A relative. Well, you know."

"Absolutely. Your fiduciary responsibility doesn't extend to keeping secrets."

"Oh, secrets." The man laughed, a single mild guffaw. "But you know, that Parker cabin."

Paul waited, uncertain. When the man did not continue, Paul said, "No. Is it a historical place?"

"No." The man felt his sweater and chuckled shortly. "No, not historical. Except to stretch the meaning. Some pioneers died up there of cholera. You can see the graves if you look around. That's hardly major history."

Paul felt a twitch of impatience, but smiled.

"Except to stretch the meaning all out of shape," the man said slowly, with a strangely unpleasant expression on his face. "It's not the sort of place you would see a whole lot about in any of the guide books. But it's a very remarkable place."

"Tell me more about it."

The man looked beyond Paul, out the window, watching the rain. "A charming place. Remote. Hard to get to. And very picturesque. Native stone. Fireplace." As he spoke he did not seem to be thinking the words he was saying, but other, much different words.

"Is there anything else especially remarkable about it?"

"Hardly anyone's ever heard of it." The man smiled in a fatherly way. "Hardly anyone. I was glad to have a tenant for it."

"Is there anything unusual about the house?"

"It's an unusual house."

"In what way, exactly?"

"In a wide variety of ways. A wide, wide variety of ways."

"I see," said Paul dryly.

Ed pulled his lip, and said, after a long while, "So nobody's heard a lick from this cousin of yours in two months?"

"That's right."

The two large, pale hands tugged open a drawer and took out a small manila envelope. The envelope opened with a snap. A brass key gleamed in the suddenly much brighter light from the desk lamp.

"Just continue on up to Calistoga. Take the county road, two-lane, like you were going to the coast." The complexity of the instructions, or a distracting thought, brought silence. He picked up a pen. "I'll draw you a map."

The pen scarred a sheet of paper without a sound. Paul took the paper and thanked Ed, shaking his hand.

"And you might drop by the sheriff. Drop on by and say hello, how are you doing today, that sort of thing."

"The sheriff."

"Couldn't hurt. And take your time, maybe spend the night in Calistoga. Start out tomorrow morning. Those little county roads just aren't what they could be, you know."

"That sounds like good advice."

"And you can get yourself some pretty good food in Calistoga. Really have yourself some good food in quite a lot of places up there; maybe you know about all that."

Paul said that he did.

"But you really ought to go out there tomorrow. In the morning."

Paul said that he would, and hurried through the rain to the car.

Lise wanted to know what had happened. "What did you talk about? I thought you'd just pop in and pop out with the key."

"I did."

"You sat there talking to him."

"I couldn't just snatch it and run away."

"What did he say?"

"You know these guys who spend all day sitting alone in an office. They like to talk."

The vineyards on either side of the road were rust-black in the rain. The hills of the valley vanished into the low clouds. The wipers struggled to clear the glass of the rain that fell in huge splatters. Paul turned on the headlights and a pheasant broke across the road. The white ring around its neck was brilliant, and then the bird was gone.

"Beautiful," said Lise, but her voice was joyless. Perhaps because they could have hit the bird, Paul thought, although it had not been even close. Perhaps because of some private thought that troubled her.

"I thought we'd spend the night in Calistoga," Paul said.

"Oh, that sounds wonderful," she replied, and Paul was surprised at how happy she was.

9

Paul poured them both some zinfandel, and sighed. He was glad at last to be in a simple restaurant, a place that served magnificent hamburgers and golden onion rings, and simple red wine. It even had a fireplace of artificial stone and a fire of concrete logs and a pipe that squirted flames.

Sometimes, sitting across a table from Lise like this, he felt so happy he could not believe it.

He had reviewed this restaurant three years before, when he had done a series on the perfect hamburger. It still served a perfect hamburger, four stars, and still had the plain ambience that Paul found himself loving. He examined the burst of parsley on his plate, and, smiling at Lise, ate it.

Apple pie would be too perfect, so he took a deep breath and ordered cheesecake. It was hard to tell whether or not the coffee had been filtered, perked, or simmered in a skillet. For once, he did not mind at all. It was hot, and it tasted good.

The bartender glanced his way, and Paul sensed interest from the swinging door of the kitchen. "I don't go in for the gourmet hamburger. Those fancy burgers on sourdough, with artichoke hearts, or whatever. I like a simple burger. Like this."

"Simple food, for a simple guy," Lise suggested, with a mischievous smile.

Lise was having strawberry ice cream. They both seemed to enjoy their escape from good taste.

"I think anything done well is worth admiring. Even something normal, like good cheesecake. And this is delicious."

But he knew that one of the reasons he enjoyed this food so much was Lise. It was a good thing he would not have to review this restaurant. He would probably give it maniacal praise.

"Maybe we ought to slip back into good taste for a moment," said Paul.

"And ruin a perfect meal?"

"I know. It's a bad idea. But aren't the gods supposed to dislike perfection among mortals? Maybe some cognac."

"I've never cared for cognac," she said.

This struck Paul as very sad, and he considered her in a new light.

She guessed that he was troubled, and suggested, "You don't like this place."

The table was being cleared, and all ears were, no doubt, tuned to his voice. "I like it," he said, "I like it a lot. What is it you don't like about cognac?"

"The flavor, I suppose."

This was tough news. The flavor was the very best thing about cognac. He ordered a snifter for himself, and some Kahlua over ice for Lise, and tried not to think about the dream. The way his legs could not move. The way his head could not turn.

"The only thing I can think of not to like about cognac," he said, "is the color."

"But look at it! It's beautiful!"

He sipped. "Not real. Caramel coloring is added. I have often wondered what it would look like uncolored. Pale, I suppose, maybe even very pale, like vodka with a dash of bitters."

"I hate it when they add color to things. I like to see what's really there."

"You're in the wrong place, at the wrong time. Kahlua has added color. So does Coca-Cola. Everything. The whole world is tricked out, just the tiniest bit fake. And I wish it weren't, but I can't get too upset about it."

They strolled along the sidewalk, as long as awnings protected them from rain. Lise stayed close to him, in a way that made him happy. He put his arm around her. The street was empty. Orange leaves the size of baseball mitts floated in puddles.

"Doesn't it seem odd that we have to travel from home in order to feel happy?" she asked.

She surprised him often in the things she said. She truly was more intelligent than he was, although perhaps not smarter. He thought of smarts as the ability to get things done. Intelligence was the ability to consider, and the ability to love.

He knew she loved her studies, but did she love him? And if she did, would she marry him? He had taken too long to respond to her question, so he said, "Do you think it's wrong to want to see new places?"

"No, it's a good thing, but why do we have to?"

He didn't know. He didn't know himself, and he didn't know her. He was very ignorant. But at least he wasn't a fool. He didn't sit up all night in graveyards, trying to take pictures of a ghost.

As he emerged from the bathroom, he was puzzled to see her reading the Bible from the nightstand. But why not? She probably had spiritual depths he could not dream of. This thought made him feel quiet, and small.

"We're having an adventure!" he said.

She closed the book, and looked at him, as if frightened.

"We shouldn't think so much," he said. "We shouldn't be so serious. This is an exciting time." He plunged back into the bathroom and made a hood out of a towel.

He turned off the light, and slowly opened the door.

"Paul, you're scaring me."

He did not move.

"Paul, stop it. You're scaring me."

He held his breath.

"Paul, stop it and come out of there this very minute or I'll never forgive you."

He opened the door a little more, and crouched low, sticking his head into the darkness.

"Paul, God damn it!" she cried, and Paul swooped across the room in a flutter of towel, unable to tackle her as she eluded him and ducked behind the television set.

Paul laughed until he had to sit on the bed, and flicked the towel at her. "I scared you," he wheezed.

"You're a total maniac," she said, mussing his hair.

"I want to be a ghost again."

"An absolute, complete maniac. You ought to be in an institution." She bit his ear, enough to hurt.

"You're crazy, too. Afraid of someone wearing a towel."

"Afraid of someone who's hopelessly silly."

"I'm sure ghosts are very silly, too. They'd almost have to be. Wouldn't you be silly if you walked around looking like a length of toilet paper all the time?"

"Seriously?"

"Sure."

"The mistake," she said, "is thinking of a ghost as the residue of a dead person. Like a sheath of wrapping paper left in a place where the person was murdered, for example. A spirit left to wander, like Hamlet's father. That we can set aside. We have to see the ghost as something quite separate. As a thing that perhaps was never a person at all."

"Silliness," he said, slipping the strap from her nightie. She stood, and her nightgown pooled on the floor, looking like a husk a spirit might leave behind, diaphanous trash, impossible, naturally, as ghosts were impossible.

He woke early the next morning, ran the electric shaver over his chin, and slipped out of the motel alone. He had imagined a day blazing and clear, if not warm at least crisp and cloudless. He jammed his hands into his pockets, and considered going back into the room for his raincoat.

Instead, he ran across the street, and around the corner. A single policeman read a newspaper behind a desk. As always at the sight of a newspaper, Paul wondered if this was one of his issues.

"Help you?"

"You aren't the sheriff, are you?"

"No. Sheriff would be back in Saint Helena. A problem?"

The cop had an angular face, like wood carved quickly to resemble a human head. Paul liked the way the cop happily put aside the newspaper, which Paul saw was merely a local, and leaned forward with at least a show of interest.

Paul explained his search for his cousin, making it all sound off-hand, which it was. He mentioned that the realtor had suggested checking in with the authorities, and here he was. Not the right authorities, though, they both agreed.

"County jurisdiction would definitely be the sheriff. Give him a call. Have a sheriff meet you out there. They'd be glad to help."

He was a friendly cop, and made Paul imagine for a moment that just maybe a sheriff would be glad to drive for miles on a country road to help look for a fool, but explaining the cousin to the policemen, with a policeman's Mr. Coffee in one corner, and a silent but competent-looking police radio in the other, made Paul realize how thin the problem was, how silly, and how puny compared with the problems police usually faced.

He left the police station feeling refreshed. And manly, too. He had seen a cop. The cop had listened seriously. The cop had said other cops would listen seriously and be equally friendly. The cop had wished him a good day, and meant it.

He would not bother these police, with their shotguns and short-wave radios. He felt confident, now, and strode back to the motel room, oblivious to the rain.

Lise rubbed a towel into her hair. "Where'd you go?"

He shrugged his shoulders to ease the clammy shirt off his skin for a moment. "I dropped into the police station."

"Oh?"

"Just thought I'd check in with them. Let them know what we were up to."

"What did they say?"

"Not much." He swaggered around the room. "I mean, what could they say? My cousin is obviously just a silly twerp who's off in the woods doing something city people do. Taping ghosts. Or screwing goats." He laughed.

She gave him a steady look.

"Well, I just thought I'd check in with them."

He felt less confident now. The macho glow faded from him, and he wished that she were as buoyant as he had been, just to make him feel better.

He should call the sheriff, he thought. The thought hit him like a slap. As foolish as it sounded, it was the right thing to do.

They breakfasted in a café with a long counter crowded with men in straw cowboy hats. Most of them seemed to know each other, and it took a long time to get served. The coffee was tasteless, the sort of coffee of which it is said, "tasteless but hot." But it was too hot at first, and rapidly cooled.

The hash browns were leathery, and Paul recalled horror stories of hash browns that were dried and packaged, and reconstituted with water just before use. He wasn't sure what had happened to these hash browns, but they were grim. The eggs were watery— sunny-side-up does not mean raw. The sausage was as sad a length of gut as Paul had ever seen.

"I've never hit on the right breakfast to order at a place like this. Pancakes, maybe, but they always make me feel peculiar. Too full, too jittery. The syrup, I guess. And thirsty. But you can't really ruin pancakes, can you? Or griddle cakes, as they call them on this menu."

"What will we do if we get there and there's no food?"

Paul put down his fork. "Of course there will be food. Or a grocery somewhere."

"You believe that when we get there your cousin will be frying lambchops in the kitchen with some sort of muscular lover. He'll be put off at first, but gradually happy to have us."

Paul didn't know what to say. This had, in fact, been his fantasy. Or that perhaps he would have cameras set up all over the grounds of the place, whatever it looked like. But that certainly he would have food.

"It's a terrible thing to take food."

"Why?" she asked.

"It's an admission that he might not be there. If he's not there, we have problems."

"If he's not there, we stay and wait. We'll have a vacation."

That seemed a little coldhearted, but the thought appealed to Paul. "He'll be there," he said.

He peeled back the covering of a plastic tub, very small, filled with a liquid jam. It slid off his knife, so he poured it over the piece of pale toast.

He found himself hoping that there was something terrible going on at the cabin. Something challenging. Something—he bit into his toast—disturbing. Like so many people he doubted his own courage. Not that he was a cowardly person. He had simply never been tested. This little visit to the woods might turn out to be exactly the right sort of test.

A man in a green plastic poncho strode into the café, water trailing him in a ragged line of glistening drops. He greeted the man behind the counter, and they both agreed that it was indeed raining.

Perhaps, Paul thought, it was foolish to want to be tested. He chewed his toast. He did not often indulge in self-analysis. He knew too many people who thought about themselves constantly. They pondered their religious beliefs, or lack of same, their sex lives, or lack of same, and as a result they couldn't think about anything concrete. They had opinions instead of thoughts. When he talked to them he could tell they were poised on the edge of speech, ready to leap forward with a comment of their own, not listening at all to what was being said.

Paul listened. He tasted. He paid attention to the details around him. He tried to be a glass the world passed through without change in color or form. He prided himself on his objectivity, and on his interest in the world around him. He was curious, in a world of people who had little interest in anything but themselves.

It was annoying the way the world had begun to repeat itself. People he had never met before said the things he had heard too often, smiled the same cocky smiles, shook hands in the same way, self-assertive and painfully likable, laughing too quickly, too quick to admire the canapés.

People were greedy for money and power, but also for something even more elusive: more of themselves. More good looks, more comfort, a better view. So that they could own more of a human life than before, as if they were characters on television whose destinies led them into higher levels of self-assurance, and nothing more.

A glass between them was crammed with paper packets of sugar.

Paul extricated one from the clutch. It was decorated with a picture of the Golden Gate Bridge. He knew that if he examined the others he would see views of different landmarks. Already he could see the Grand Canyon, and a white plume which had to be, he guessed, Old Faithful.

"Will there be anything else?" asked the waitress.

Why did Paul think, "Yes, there will be much more. I never want to leave this place"?

He said simply that he did not want anything else. Men at the counter laughed and blew on their coffee and drank it, and outside the rain covered the street with a white stubble that shifted and rippled, like a vision of something that was not real.

10

Lise handed Paul a sandwich wrapped in plastic. Tuna the color and consistency of peanut butter grinned at him from between the slices of bread. Paul sidled close to her, not wanting anyone else in the grocery store to hear him. "Can't we get something a little better than this?"

"I want to have a picnic."

"We can't have a picnic. It's pouring!"

"We'll huddle somewhere."

It almost sounded inviting, Paul admitted to himself, admiring the way she replaced one orange and selected another. "I've been on some great picnics," said Paul. "There can be problems, though. Pine needles always fall on something you're eating."

She plucked the sandwich from his hand. She tossed it onto a pile of identical, sealed packages of white bread and gluey filling. Paul picked it up again. "I'm sorry. If you want to have a picnic, we'll have a picnic. I'll find some cheese. One of those nice Camemberts they make around here. And a wine of some sort. We can—" He pictured them huddled in the rain. "We can find someplace where it's not raining so hard."

"We are supposed to be having a vacation, after all," she said.

"That's right. And everyone knows you have picnics all the time on vacations."

"I was reading the Song of Solomon last night. 'O that you would kiss me with the kisses of your mouth! For your love is better than wine.' And I wanted to have a picnic. And there's no reason to be chained by the weather. We can do whatever we want to do."

"Do you often read the Bible?"

"I read everything I can get my hands on," she answered. "I read Freud in the sixth grade, hiding the book from my parents and the teacher because it mentioned things like vaginas and masturbation. And, of course, the phallus."

Paul glanced around. One did not, exactly, say "vagina" or "phallus" in a grocery store in Calistoga. A wrinkled man in a straw cowboy hat sniffed the end of a cantaloupe.

"And recently working on Donne's sermons, I've read a good deal of the Bible. King James, not that claptrap Revised Standard stuff."

She was an amazing countryside of knowledge. He felt ignorant, and hefted a bunch of bananas to recover his self-assurance. Surely he could not ask such an amazing creature to marry him. He wasn't a total idiot. Far from it. But she had depths. He was a shiny, sparkling stretch of water children could wade in, and sail paper boats. She was a river of unexplored shoals and depths.

She looked into his eyes, impossibly beautiful. "The Bible is so self-contradictory. I think the most important things are."

Paul nodded thoughtfully, and selected a slender bottle of rosé.

He drove to the edge of a vineyard, and then, carefully, very nearly into it. He turned off the engine, and the rain was loud on the car roof.

They did not get out of the car, but they opened the doors so that it felt like a picnic. Paul gouged the cork with the corkscrew of his Swiss Army knife. Bits of cork bobbed in the wine by the time he wrestled the bottle open, and he reminded himself never to use that particular corkscrew again.

The Camembert was barely ripe, but it suited the wine. They sipped from Styrofoam while a blackbird stared at them from the chimney of a smudge pot, then looked away, as if they belonged exactly where they were.

"See, these sandwiches aren't so bad," Lise said, chewing happily.

Paul swallowed a mass of mucilage, flavored faintly with tuna.

"I love picnics," she breathed. "I suppose it's the only speck of romanticism in me."

"This is what they call a pointed rebuke."

"No, it's the truth."

The wind gusted rain into the car for a moment. The grass among the grapevines was neon green, and a crow crawled slowly across the sky.

"Besides," Paul said, "there's a lot of romantic in you."

"Not as much as you think."

"Not as little as you think. That's what I like about you. You're a little bit of everything, but not in a sloppy, tossed-together way. You're very accomplished."

"I took piano lessons once," she mused. "I hated them."

"Everyone hates piano lessons. I suppose even great pianists hate actually sitting down and practicing. It's something they have to do to do what they like."

"Which is?"

Paul chewed his sandwich, and chased it quickly with a gulp of rosé. "Performing, I suppose. What do I know about pianists?"

Perhaps it was the feeling that she was enjoying herself, or the flush of wine so early in the day, or the fact that he didn't really mind sitting in a small car in the middle of a vineyard, but he chose that moment to unravel the subject he had been keeping to himself. "We've been seeing each other for a couple of years," he began.

She rolled the sandwich wrapper into a ball, and sipped her wine.

"Off and on," he continued.

"Mostly on," she said, in what sounded like an encouraging tone.

"Mostly." Except for a man built like a bear, a bearded astronomer she had gone rafting with once. Paul didn't think anything significant had passed between the bear and Lise, which is to say he couldn't imagine them in bed.

Paul couldn't talk. It wasn't going at all well. He should have begun talking about it last night, or much later, before a crackling fire. But he had begun, and he had to continue.

"And I've decided," he said in a rush, "that it might be best if after all this time seeing each other we actually went ahead and got married."

He could not look at her. Rain drooled down the windshield, and a crow laughed slowly in a stand of trees.

The nakedness of what he had said coiled between them. Paul wrapped what was left of his sandwich, and looked away from her, watching water drop gently off the snaking branches of the grapevines.

Her hand was on his hand, and then she held him, as well as she could with the gearshift jabbing them like a robot's erection. She breathed into his ear, and he held her, but then she drew back. "I knew you were going to ask me," she said. "I don't know how, but I could tell." She was blushing, and he had never seen her blush before. He thought it was with pleasure.

"What do you think?" he asked, hoarsely.

"It's wonderful that you should mention it," she began.

Paul held his breath.

"And in a very strange and wonderful way, I feel honored."

Paul waited.

"Because certainly if I were thinking of marrying anyone, it would be you."

Paul exhaled very slowly.

She looked away, and he followed her gaze through the bleary windshield toward the perfect gray sky. "A long time ago I decided how I was going to live my life. I was just a girl, walking home from the library with books that I really wasn't going to understand very well at all. Darwin. Milton. Melville. Anything I could get my hands on that I had heard grown-ups mention, or had read about in the encyclopedia, I wanted to read. And I decided that someday I would be a scholar, and know practically everything there was to know."

The steering wheel was cold, and the chill that surrounded the car breathed slowly into it.

"Naturally, it was difficult. Both of my parents were basically undereducated. High school, period, and not very sophisticated high school. I don't think college is the only way to get an education, but my father doesn't even know who Milton, or Keats, or Dickens were. Never even heard of them. And my mother's idea of good writing is a little collection of Hallmark inspirational verse, the sort of book with cartoon lambs cavorting in it, and butterflies with smiling faces. Butterflies, for Christ's sake. Smiling insects!"

Paul opened his mouth to stop her, but words fled him.

"Neither one of them was at all interested in my going to college, and I had to work my way, as you know, hauling linen out of motel rooms, and pouring coffee for lechers. I'm not complaining. But I finally got a grant to do graduate work and nail a PhD, and nothing is going to stop me."

"But someday . . ." Paul began.

"Someday, soon, I'll have my dissertation polished off, and then I'll go to teach at maybe Stanford, I don't know. Or stay at Cal; I think they might want me. I have connections at Yale. Former professors who swear they would kill for me. I've made a good impression." She spoke wistfully, as if she were not quite sure it was all true. "Of course, I don't know everything. I have studied myself to the point that I know the extent of my ignorance."

Paul knew about ignorance. He seemed to suffer from it most of the time. He suffered from it now, not knowing what to say to the woman he suddenly loved more than ever.

"I have never thought in terms of marriage. I have given myself over to becoming a scholar, as if I were becoming a nun."

"You've scarcely been celibate," Paul murmured.

"If I misled you, I'm sorry." She shook, weeping. "I don't want to hurt you, Paul. I just can't say yes."

Paul ground his forehead into the steering wheel, wishing that its hard, cold strength could help him. "I don't want to hurt your career. Our marriage would not do the slightest little harm to your profession. You could go on learning, and we can move anywhere. I'm sick of my job, anyway."

She looked away, trembling.

"All right. I won't press it. God knows, it took me so long to mention it, I'll probably never say another word about it. I don't want you to say no, and then feel that you have to stick to that answer out of stubbornness. You like to make up your mind what you're going to do, and then go right ahead and do it. I appreciate that. More than that, I admire it. You are the most remarkable woman—the most remarkable person—I have ever met. I think, hell I don't know what I think anymore. I want you to be happy. I want us to be together. So promise me this—you'll think about it. Okay? You won't say for sure one way or another, but you'll think about it. Will you?"

She nodded, blinking. "I'll think."

"Good. Good. You'll think. I'll settle for that for the time being."

"But you promise me something."

"What?"

"That you won't mention the subject until I say you can."

Paul controlled a quick response, and said carefully, "I can wait."

"And you won't give me meaningful, searching looks. We can just go ahead and have a nice little time away from everything, just like we had planned."

"Sure. We'll pretend like this conversation never happened. If that's what you want."

But it was clear to Paul that while Lise liked him, and was "honored" by his love for her, she was not quite as fond of him as he was of her. Oh, they were good friends. And lovers, and very affectionate. But she would rather be a scholar. It made her, in a way, all the more alluring. The scholar as beauty.

"I'm glad to be away from it," she said. "People think of academia as an ivory tower, but it's more like a factory. People slicing poets thinner and thinner, representations of self in Herbert, introspection in Marvell, the influence of Dante on the Romantics. Not that these studies don't matter. But that the motive for performing the erudition is to acquire a more lustrous name, so you can move to a better university, get more money, buy a better car. Like those experiments on mice they do over and over again. Everyone knows if you make a white mouse drink a half liter of vodka a day something funny will happen to it, but they pop open thousands and thousands of animals so they can whip their livers into pâté and look at them under a microscope. I think of the poets as mice, only thank God they can't be hurt, even the living ones, if they have any sense."

The mice had something to do with the two of them, but Paul was not sure what. Her weariness with her studies had somehow made her tired of everything, even love. Or not love, exactly, but commitment. She had taken on so much that she could not stand any more demands.

"You'll be a magnificent professor," Paul said. "You'll become the most incredible thing that ever hit the academic swamp."

"I don't want to be incredible. Just competent."

"You'll be great."

"The competition is appalling."

"Terrible, or very good?"

She smiled wanly. "Very good. There are about two job openings a year and about eight thousand brilliant crazed animals struggling to get in."

He wanted to tell her: anything, anywhere. I will do anything for you.

He shifted the car into neutral without starting it, and wobbled the gear shift back and forth for a moment. "We'll have lots of picnics," he said.

He started the car. He eased the car over the uneven gravel road, as if the birds that peppered the spaces between the rows of grape vines were all the ways that he could lose her. He drove carefully, deliberately, so they would not take flight.

11

The road twisted through vineyards, some vines ancient with black, arthritic stumps, others new, youthful vines on glistening black stakes. The road cut along hills, and looped across bridges over creeks of high water. The creeks were cocoa-brown with runoff and boiled over boulders like huge skulls.

Paul enjoyed the drive. He had driven this part before, and dodged the occasional pothole easily. He enjoyed the drive so much he had to step on the brake and back up. "We missed the turnoff," he said.

This road was different. Trees whispered over the top of the car in places, and water dripped from their branches in irregular splatters. Vineyards, when they were visible, were rows of black fists in wedge-shaped parcels of land. The rare house was a plume of chimney smoke from the crotch of a hill.

The houses grew more rare, and the hills were steep on both sides of the road, as the road narrowed, a thin paste of asphalt over rough stones. A sheep stood in the middle of the road, and Paul stopped the car, rolling down the window to say hello to it. The sheep shied away, and ran, leaping a barbed-wire fence.

Paul turned up a gravel road, past a sign that said: McCorckle Vineyards—Tasting. The car lurched along the gravel, and Paul pulled into a yard plastered with wet leaves, and the debris of unharvested walnuts.

He answered Lise's unasked question. "This isn't the way. I just wanted to stop for a while."

It wasn't quite that simple. As he drove he found it impossible to stop thinking about the dream, and the trip seemed more and more wrong. He had to stop to rest his hands, which were numb from gripping the wheel. He needed contact with a stranger, someone casual whom he would never see again, to restore his calm.

A gray horse watched from behind a fence. Paul walked over to the horse, telling the horse that he was pleased to meet it. The animal watched with quiet, black eyes, but when Paul tried to pat the center of its forehead, the animal flinched, and backed away.

"Nervous," Paul explained, miffed.

A figure was watching from a doorway. The figure shrank back into darkness as they approached. They consoled each other that horses around here might not see many people, but Paul knew that they must see enough people not to be easily frightened.

They stepped into the protection of a large, aluminum-sided warehouse, and as they slipped into the building an odor like cinnamon enveloped them. Barrels lined a wall.

"Take a look around," said a voice. A figure sidestepped into light from a yellow bulb. Paul had expected a sturdy, older man. Instead he faced a thin young man, who held his place in a book with a finger.

There was, really, nowhere to look. Stainless steel tanks gleamed among shadows, and a drain grinned in the center of the concrete floor.

The young man touched the lip of a copper basin. A residue as dark as blood reflected the yellow of the bulb, a mustard-bright smear. The finger slipped out of the book, and the slit in the pages closed, as if forever.

"Taste?" said the young man.

"Of course," said Paul, although he did not really want to taste. In this chilly dark he felt that he was being tasted, if only by salesmanship. But he put forth a hand and accepted a hock glass brilliant with a finger's-width of white wine.

"We start with the dry, and work up toward the sweet," said the young man. How else? thought Paul, but he sipped, pursed his lips and spat into the copper basin. It was the sort of basin typical of ambitious wineries. A bowl the size of a medieval shield, it rested on a table to receive the wine a taster might not want to swallow.

A pause. A response was required before the wine could be named. Paul knew how to respond in a dozen ways. He knew how to charm. But what was charm but the ability to beguile, the ability to lie? Paul wanted to be honest. "Pleasant," he said. "A little effervescence. But a little thin."

"That is our driest wine," said the young man.

Paul turned, as if addressing Lise, who was in the act of spitting into the basin herself. "It's easy to mistake lack of taste for dryness," he said. But he stopped himself, immediately regretting his honesty. "But it has its good points. A good food wine."

The young man relaxed slightly, and his hand closed around the neck of another bottle. "This is a young red."

Black wine glittered in the glass. Paul did not taste it at once. He did not want to taste wine. It was a liquid that was ripe with magic, with the power to ease. He did not want to be eased. It was just another way of pretending. He wanted truth. He sipped, and spat.

"Petite Sirah," said the young man. "Where are you two headed?"

"West of here, toward the coast," Paul said.

The young man picked up the next bottle.

"And then off the main road—if you can call this road a main road. To a place called the Parker cabin."

"Let me give you fresh glasses."

"These are fine."

"It doesn't matter. We get so few visitors. One other couple, maybe two, all day yesterday."

With a touch of nausea Paul considered that the spat wine in the copper basin was thrown out only every day or two. They both accepted new glasses of a hideously sweet white wine. Paul nodded, and half-missed the basin. "Sweet," he said, like a man saying "Shit."

"Our sauterne."

"I like it!" said Lise.

"Yes, it's by far our most popular," said the young man, but his voice was without interest.

Paul asked after prices, and admired the color of the first wine—"like mountain air," whatever that meant—and then asked, "Have you heard of the Parker cabin?"

This was a crude way of asking, but Paul was not in the mood for building up to inquiry. The young man touched the mouth of a bottle thoughtfully. "I don't know," he said.

Paul took out his wallet. He selected a few bills, and laid them on the table beside the copper basin. "We'll have a couple bottles of the sauterne," he said.

"A good choice," said the young man, rummaging in a box. "Most of it comes from the vineyards you see around here. We are very proud of it."

It was pathetic to be proud of such an insipid wine, thought Paul. Or perhaps pride itself was pitiful. Any pride, in anything. "It's an isolated place, this Parker cabin. I'm not sure I have the directions right."

The young man took the hand-drawn map. He held it under the light. He folded the map, pressing the crease hard with his fingers before handing it back. "That'll get you there."

"I hear it's a pretty colorful place," suggested Paul.

"Be careful on those roads," said the young man.

"I hear it's a place with a lot of history."

"A lot of places like that around here."

The young man evidently wanted to return to his book. Paul tucked the two bottles under his arm. They clanked together, and the wine in them made an alto gurgle, like strange, distant music.

"There is a lot of history in a lot of places around here," said the young man, and for the first time it was clear to Paul that this man knew something he was not telling. But he was so reticent, so eager to read, or so hungry for silence, that he was unlikely to say much more. Paul did not believe that there was a great deal of history in these red-rocked hills. Not, at least, much human history.

"Be real careful on those roads," said the young man at the door.

"They're very slick," said Lise.

"It's not the roads so much. You just want to be real careful."

"We'll be careful," said Lise.

The young man hesitated, wanting, apparently, to warn them about something, but not wanting to seem unfriendly. "Some bad things have happened up at the cabin, but that was all a long time ago. You'll have a good time."

The horse watched them from the middle of the pasture. It did not move, standing with its four legs in gray grass, with just the beginnings of new, green growth far beneath the dead fuzz. As they drove back to the road, the horse turned to watch them. Its tail hung straight down, dark in the suddenly heavy rain.

Paul felt that he had to say something to dispel what the young man had said. "I'm beginning to think that people who work alone become a little peculiar."

"Oh, him," said Lise, dismissively. "He was just a strange young man."

Lise clutched the map. Paul drove slowly. Water spilled over the road, and the wipers flailed against the downpour.

"This is it!" cried Lise, at last.

They turned up an even narrower road, the Volkswagen struggling through potholes. Paul shifted into first as the road worked its way over a hill, then wended through a stand of bay trees dropping yellow, graceful leaves.

Paul drove for an age, growing gradually incredulous. "How much farther can it be?"

"The map is inconclusive as to distances," said Lise, in a professorial manner.

"Len must have been insane to move all the way out here," Paul said. "I've never seen such a terrible road."

"It's probably pretty at other times of the year."

"Give me the map!" He stopped the car, and wrenched the handbrake into position. "We have to cross a bridge. The cabin is just beyond that."

"I could have told you that."

"I'm sorry. I just can't believe this."

Lise accepted the map with a slightly hurt expression. "I'll tell you how we're doing. Just keep driving."

Paul released the brake. "I can't help feeling we're lost."

The road had slumped away at some points, and Paul had to maneuver the car over rocks, until the road resumed. At last a creek roared under a bridge of hairy logs and pale, gray planks.

"We should be there," said Lise, as the car rattled across the bridge.

Paul got out of the car. Redwoods shivered in the wind, and redwood needles had turned the ground tobacco-brown as far as he could see. The road ended, abruptly, after the bridge. Paul understood that this was the end of the journey, but he could see no cabin. He could see no sign of human beings at all.

He untangled a nylon raincoat, put it on, and huffed his way up a long slope through the redwood trees. The trees pattered the ground with gentle drops of water, as the heavy rain filtered its way through them, becoming peaceful. There was great quiet, except for the sound of the drops of water padding on the needle-carpeted ground.

When he saw it, he stood, amazed. A small cabin, built of round, gray stones. Dark windows stared out at him, and the chimney was a lifeless stump. Paul backed away from it, until a tree nudged him from behind.

He ran down the slope, back to the car.

"Did you see him?" Lise asked, pulling on her raincoat.

Paul picked up his suitcase, and gathered a load of groceries under his arm. "No." But he added quickly, "I didn't really go up to it. I didn't want to leave you alone in the car."

"Can't we drive any closer?"

"No. It's surrounded by trees."

They walked, each carrying a load, through the dripping water. "It's beautiful!" she said when she saw it. "Such a charming cabin. I'm so glad it's not built of logs. And that it's not one of those hideous A-frames."

"Built of native stone," Paul said. The words sounded cheering, somehow.

Lise deposited her suitcase on the front step. "It's really fairly large, when you get up to it. Look, it has a second story."

Paul tried the door, which did not even creak, it was so firmly locked. He drew back his hand. What disturbed him was that he had not bothered to knock. Without thinking, he had assumed the place was empty. And there was something else he had not bothered to think about: there was no other car.

"I don't think he's here," said Lise.

"I don't think so either," said Paul, fishing the key from his pocket. He slipped the key into the slot, but did not turn it at once.

"Hurry. We can't stand out here in the rain all afternoon."

He turned the key, and the door opened silently.

There was a tangle of half-burned logs in the blackened fireplace. A deer head thrust from the wood-paneled wall above a disheveled sofa. Newspapers were scattered across the floor, and a hatchet was sunk deep into a block of wood.

"It's cold in here," said Lise. Their breath made wisps of vapor before them.

"I'll build a fire," said Paul. He stood before the fireplace. It was a source of great cold. He knelt, and crumpled a sheet of newspaper. The date in the corner was weeks past. He wadded the paper tightly, and found some scraps of blond wood to thrust under the charred logs.

The act of lighting the newspaper with a wooden match released some tension in him. He watched the fire spill across the newspaper, and pause like a living thing at the first shard of wood. The wood shrank, and a bright flame rose like a blade from its heart.

"It will be much cheerier when that gets going," he said.

"Oh, I think it's very cheery as it is. Cozy, even. We'll have a little vacation out here in the woods, where no one in the world can bother us."

"Why not?" Paul was eager for the solitude, and now that a fire snapped in the fireplace, he felt the absence of his cousin much less.

"It's a large kitchen," he called. "Propane stove. Big and black, maybe a modified wood-burner." Water burst from the tap. "Good water pressure." He shook a tin of oregano, and stopped.

On the table, beside an empty cup, was a camera. He stood over it for a long while before he could touch it. It was cold, as was everything else. And heavy. Paul knew nothing about cameras, but it seemed expensive. He held it like a gun, and put it down gingerly.

He opened the small refrigerator. A single can of beer remained in the plastic loops of a six-pack. A jar of mustard. Some frozen dinners in the freezer. Paul closed the door quickly.

"It's warm!" said Lise happily, her back against the fireplace. "You make a good fire."

"We have to do something unpleasant," said Paul.

Her expression grew serious when she saw his look. "What's the matter?"

"We have to do something maybe even horrible."

"What on earth?"

"I don't think Len is gone."

"Of course he's gone."

Paul shook his head.

"He's not here. No car, no nothing. What are you talking about?"

"There's a camera in the kitchen. One of those expensive Leicas. He wouldn't leave a piece of equipment like that."

"I might."

"No, you wouldn't. And if you did, you'd come back for it."

"What are you saying?"

Paul did not speak.

"He's gone. He's not here."

Paul looked up, at the ceiling. "I'm looking upstairs." He did not move at once, but waited, he did not know for what.

"This isn't funny," said Lise. "I don't know what's the matter with you."

Paul put his hand on a hand-hewn banister. A step accepted his weight without creaking.

"Stop creeping around, for Christ's sake," said Lise, crossing her arms. "You're jumping to conclusions."

Paul took the steps slowly. "I don't jump to conclusions," he said.

All the doors opened onto the landing. He touched the first doorknob, which was icy. The door revealed an expanse of green linoleum, and a sloppily arrayed throw rug, the sort of fabric that reminded Paul of tripe.

He hooked a finger and slowly drew back the gray shower curtain. A tube of shampoo. A rust-freckled drain grill. A washcloth folded neatly over a rail, and a bar of green soap. A toothbrush waited on the sink, beside a tube of toothpaste with its cap on tight.

Paul could not breathe. He opened the cabinet, and had to touch the razor to be certain that it was really there.

He leaned against the wall, unable to take the next step. He regretted accepting this errand of responsibility, this kindness to a favorite aunt. Move, he commanded himself. Do what you have to do.

The bedroom was tidy. A bed was made neatly, and an assortment of books was lined across the dresser. Paperbacks, mostly. Books about photography, and books of paintings by Monet and Turner. Art criticism. The sort of books a person would enjoy having nearby, without looking at them very often.

Clothes hung in the closet. Wool shirts, and jeans which had been neatly ironed. A pair of hiking boots gaped beside a pair of slippers. He glanced under the bed.

The bedroom opposite was a naked place. An army cot had been set up in the corner, and the closet was empty, except for a single metal hanger, which hung from its hook like a thing that was not really there, an abstraction of an idea, a mathematical proof. Paul touched it, and it swung back and forth without a sound.

"I looked in the downstairs bedroom," Lise called from the stairs. She backed down the steps when she saw the look in Paul's eyes. Paul was silent.

"What is it?" she whispered.

"He's not here," he said.

She relaxed against the banister. "You frightened me!"

"But there's something wrong. His toothbrush, his toothpaste. Everything is here."

"He went for a walk. He'll be back soon."

"Maybe." Paul hurried into the downstairs bedroom, eager to be reassured. A photographer's tripod gleamed in the middle of the room, and a cassette tape recorder sat in the center of a card table. A microphone poised on a stand, pointed upward, toward the center of the ceiling. On a table in the corner gleamed a gray metal box with a padlock.

"I hate this room most of all," he said. "This equipment. This presence of interrupted activity."

"You're getting on my nerves, Paul. I don't know where he is, but this is a cozy place, and I am going to spend a few days here, curled up with a book in front of the fireplace. That's what we wanted to do, cousin or no cousin. I'm glad he's not here. It's romantic."

Paul sighed.

"We'll wait here for him," she continued. "He'll turn up. Or else he won't. Maybe he and his lover went for a fling in Reno."

"I think he was alone."

"So, he got tired of being alone and went in search of companionship. Wouldn't you?"

"Yes."

"And if you went away for a couple of days, you'd leave your cameras, wouldn't you?"

Paul shrugged. "Probably."

"We'll stay in the guest bedroom upstairs."

"It's only a cot."

"Oh, that's awkward."

"Anyway, it's a cold room. I mean, forbidding as well as chilly. We could sleep right here, in front of the fire."

"That would be wonderful. Look." She wrestled the cushions off the sofa. The piece of furniture groaned, and a mattress sprang from it, as Paul jumped away. "A sofa bed!"

"Wonderful," Paul muttered.

"Probably the first sofa bed ever manufactured, from the look of it. It smells musty. The fire will warm it up. Isn't it romantic?"

"It is indeed," Paul said, smiling with effort.

He stirred the fire with the poker.

12

There was no question about it. The cabin was romantic, and cozy, and he was happy to be standing, looking into the fire. But he found himself remembering things he had forgotten. Fragments, scraps of nightmares, fairy tales, closet doors that had to be closed before he could sleep.

It was ridiculous. He was a grown man, and he did not like feeling uneasy for no apparent reason. But he found himself remembering his one brush with horror. He had been a grown man then, too, a fledgling reporter.

Ham had assigned him to it: an exhumation.

"And we want details," Ham had said. "Not just pathos. We want to know all about it. If he's wearing a pinkie ring, we want to know about it."

Paul had driven in a daze, repeating the word to himself: *exhumation.*

A highway was being cut across the old Hanford estate, and a grave was in the way. This distinguished pioneer was being removed, to be reburied in Sacramento. All that had made sense, the way things generally did in a world which was, to a young reporter, pretty chaotic. What did not make sense was that Paul would have to watch them do it.

He parked his car at the appointed hillside, and introduced himself to a man named Franklin. Franklin worked for the county. He was an engineer, an expert on soils, including percolation tests for mineral content, if Paul understood him. "I am also," said Franklin, "by default, their head grave man."

The grave itself was marked by a headstone that was disfigured with splotches of lichen.

"And Skip here, he's a pretty fair hand with a backhoe." He indicated a young freckled man sitting without expression or apparent interest atop a yellow, earth-spattered tractor.

The engine had started, and the backhoe had flexed. And Paul had thought, trying to steady himself: Maybe it won't be so bad.

"What we want," Franklin called to Skip, "is to pull this stone out of the way."

The engine coughed. A black plume scattered in the wind. The mechanical claw jerked, unfolding through the air. It creaked, and stopped. The steel tubes that worked it telescoped in and out of themselves as the claw flexed.

When it was warmed up, the claw lowered in abrupt stages to the earth. It sawed back and forth, then lifted again. It fell with a thump, and the engine poured bruise-colored smoke into the wind.

"Can't you work it any better than that?" Franklin called.

The backhoe kid frowned.

"This is pathetic," called Franklin.

Skip's lips were tight. The ground trembled with the heavy rumble of the engine, and the arm squeaked as it lifted and fell again, working on the grass like a horse too weak to bite. The claw jumped into the air, and creaked up and down while the young man worked levers topped with black knobs. The serrated teeth of the scoop thudded into the ground, and with a rip a scoop of sod separated from the grass.

The claw hesitated. "Over there!" called Franklin.

A small amount of grass and dirt sprinkled onto the field. "Very good," called Franklin. "Now, what we want to do is pull the stone out of the way."

The claw crashed into the stone. Steel clanged against granite, and then jerked back and upward, as if injured. A white scar gouged the lichen.

Franklin bunched his fists. The claw trembled its way to the headstone and nudged it. The stone did not move. The engine rumbled, and the arm squealed. The stone moved, in the wrong direction, as if fighting the machine.

"Good," called Franklin. "You got it loose."

The claw drew back, and the headstone fell over, exposing a white, jagged root.

"Terrific," said Franklin. "Real, real good. Now you want to more or less push it along the ground there."

When the stone had been pushed, Franklin stepped to the hole it had left, and bent to peer into it. "They seated that thing in there pretty good, didn't they?"

They were silent for a moment.

Franklin made a motion with his hand. "Come on."

The hoe tore grass, lifted, dropped it.

"Try to pick up a little more with each scoop. There you go. That's doing it."

The hoe unpeeled sod, and tore it like a thick rug. The soil was black, and pale roots glistened in the drizzle. "Now we're rolling," called Franklin.

The machine worked in a slow rhythm, and Paul strolled through the grass of the field, huddled in his jacket to keep warm. When the machine was quieter, he returned, but Franklin's hand simply described the places on the surface of the field that still had to be removed, and the work continued.

At last, the engine was completely quiet. A hill of black earth had risen in the field, and Paul realized that he had forgotten how much work a machine could do.

The hole was not a tidy rectangle. It was a huge oblong, much larger than a grave, and there was no coffin visible. Nothing but dirt as dark as chocolate, and then caramel-colored dirt, scarred with the claws of the back-hoe. Franklin climbed into the hole and toed the claw marks. He forced a long, thin rod into the earth, grunting with the effort.

To Paul's horror, he withdrew the rod and sniffed it. He plunged the rod in again, and withdrew it, frowning at the tip of the rod, which was wet with earth. The third time he straightened. "We've got him."

"Rock-solid," offered Skip.

The pick rang against the side.

"Take it easy on the merchandise," said Franklin. "Dig it out up there."

Franklin wielded a shovel, stopping occasionally to blink dirt out of his eyes, or to puff out his cheeks and let air out in a slow stream. Paul felt restless watching, and vaguely guilty that he was not helping.

At last Franklin had stopped, panting. "Mahogany," he said.

"Ah," said Paul.

"Weighs a ton."

"Mmmm."

"A local product."

Paul nodded, feeling stupid. He opened his notebook and reread Franklin's full name, Berkeley Adler Franklin, and his age. Newspapers needed people's ages. Paul never understood why, but an age was always put beside a name at least once in every story he wrote. He closed the notebook.

A hawk canted overhead, scanning the field. It banked in the other direction, and glided out of sight, over the cattle that had gradually worked their way nearly over the hill.

Paul forced himself to look down. The black carapace gleamed like the exoskeleton of a cricket, smeared with yellow soil.

"We got one split," said Franklin. His forefinger made an invisible mark in the air. He looked up and made a grimace of unconcern. "Won't go anywhere."

"You're sure?" asked Paul.

"Just warped."

He crooked his finger in the direction of the machine.

The mechanical arm creaked, and the engine rumbled as the claw sawed up and down. Like the head of a huge ant, it lowered itself into the hole. "Easy," called Franklin. "You're doing great."

The mahogany husk shifted, as if by itself, and lay cradled across the steel jaw. "It's real important," called Franklin, "that you hold it just like that, all the way up. Okay?"

A nod.

"Great. Okay. Lift her up. Real good. You're looking good. You're looking real, real—okay, now that's what you have to be careful about. Oh no. Skip. Look out. It's going to fall."

It did not fall, but with a wooden grunt it slid forward, and the scoop tilted back just in time. Paul could not breathe. Franklin's hands exhorted it upward. "Come on, now, you've got it. Looking good. Ease her down. Easy. Don't jerk it down like that. Hold it!"

The metal jaw held the wooden box until it reached the ground, and then it tilted the box forward. Franklin rushed to it, and kept the box from spilling onto the grass. He walked the tractor back, and the machine was silent.

"Christ," whispered Franklin.

No one else spoke.

Franklin shook his head slowly. "That was too close for comfort, as far as I'm concerned." He stroked soil off the top of the box. "But, all's well that ends well. Where's the can opener?"

Franklin took a few steps, and picked the crowbar from the grass.

"I am," Franklin said, "surprised at the fit condition of the container. I can usually find even a very old grave by nose. But what we have here"—he grunted with effort—"is well constructed."

He gasped as he pried unsuccessfully at the lid. The wood creaked, but then was silent, and the crowbar slipped out of Franklin's hands. Paul backed away, praying that the lid would hold.

"Like I say," panted Franklin, wiping sweat and drizzle with a sleeve. "Constructed."

Skip dusted his hands against each other, and placed them on his hips, shifting so he had a good view.

Franklin held the crowbar like a pointer. "This is the workmanship of the Oakland Casket Company." He bent, and grunted. "Notice the beveled edge all the way around the lid." He grunted. "Ah. And the brass—where it's green, that's brass—hinges." He gasped and closed his eyes.

He opened his eyes. "We have it. Let's see now. Let me loosen her up down here. It's just about ready. Those hinges could use a little oil."

He stepped back.

Paul glanced, and looked away. A mouth with yellow teeth gaping wide, and a black suit. He glanced back again. That's all there was.

A skull with hair, dark and confused as a bird's nest, and a collar rich with mildew.

He walked away and did not look again.

Paul stirred the fire. Lise was singing in the kitchen. Singing a song he did not recognize, perhaps because it was in Latin, or in Middle English. He was thankful that he was able to hear Lise's voice.

Since seeing the exhumation, he had been very glad to be alive. But he had also been very careful not to remember it very clearly. Until this moment, here in this cabin, he had not really dwelled on it at all. He had typed up a quick story, one that Ham cut in half anyway, and it had been all a day's work, nothing more.

Until now.

13

Lise wanted to have the pork chops with sliced carrots for dinner, but Paul wanted spaghetti. He always prepared the dish by following a recipe he had long-since memorized. It was a meal that always seemed so hearty. "We don't want hearty," Lise said. "We want romantic."

"What's romantic about pork chops?"

"I don't know. Just trust me."

Paul zipped up his raincoat. Spaghetti was romantic, redolent as it was with those Italian herbs, and smacking of red wine. Pork chops were harmless, but uninteresting.

The rain continued, but Paul was determined to inspect the grounds of whatever place this was. He did not understand it, entirely. It was like a hunting lodge, or the weekend retreat of a prosperous but discomfort-loving businessman. It was well built. The stone walls were solid, and beautiful in this late-afternoon light. But it had an inhuman quality, as if it had erected itself out of the rock of the creekbeds without human assistance.

He walked behind the cabin, but did not get far. A creek, as loud and deep as any he had seen, ran behind the house. The cabin was on a sort of island, he realized. He followed the creek to the end of the island and stumbled over the roots of redwoods until he reached the bridge they had crossed. The Volkswagen made Paul laugh, it looked so out of place.

Everywhere the ground was tangled with roots, or heavy with half-rotted leaves. The bay trees of the creekbed were evergreen, in theory, but dropped many leaves in the autumn, and Paul gathered a handful to use in his spaghetti sauce. Fungus, which he imagined to be deadly, erupted from the bark of redwoods.

When he came upon them, they seemed to belong there, among the dripping fronds of redwood trees. He did not know what they were at first. Depressions in the earth, each the size of a narrow bed, like an army cot. Five of them, and only when he saw the headstones did he understand.

The headstones were wooden, and the words carved in them were worn invisible. There were mere indentations where there had been names, faint depressions in the harsh grain of the wood. The headstones were glazed green with moss. Paul was struck with a desire to pray.

His prayer would not be only for the dead. There was something shocking about these graves—their neglect, their solitude. Something bad, Paul thought.

Something bad had happened here.

He shook himself free of the feeling, but as he strode purposefully away from the graves, he could not help sensing that something should be done. Some act on his part was necessary; he could not guess what.

He was a great fool, he thought. He was so badly in need of a vacation, that once he began one he became preoccupied with half-digested fears. He and Lise were indeed isolated, but it was a charming isolation. The redwoods were magnificent, and if they needed to return to the civilized world for any reason, all they had to do was leap into the car and drive back across the bridge.

He entered the cabin, and did not move. Len was here, he could sense it! "Lise," he called.

"I'm here," she said, emerging from the kitchen, drying her hands on a piece of gray terrycloth. "What did you see on your walk?"

"No word from anybody?"

"No, nothing. Why?"

"I don't know. I just felt suddenly—that Len must be here."

"I'll fry him a chop in case he shows up."

"He could, you know. I almost expect him."

"He's probably back in the City visiting his mother."

74

It was possible. He might keep an alternate toothbrush there. An alternate razor. It made sense.

"What are those?"

"Bay leaves. For tomorrow night's spaghetti. The Turkish laurel is better. But the native will do nicely, if I don't use too many. Maybe half a leaf. They're full of resin. Smell."

"Wonderful!"

The wet leaves reminded him of the five sunken graves, and he could not mention them to Lise. He did not know why. They seemed brutal, somehow, or obscene. He tried to convince himself that they did not bother him, but they might bother her.

She opened one of the bottles of sauterne, and now that it was well chilled he could swallow it without too much revulsion. "I love it," she breathed, and dressed as she was in an apron she had dug out of a bottom drawer with SOUP'S ON printed on it in red letters, she was the most alluring woman he had ever seen.

"It's not too bad," he said. He touched a raw chop.

"I could stay in a place like this forever," she said.

The sentiment shocked him. "Not me. Although it's a pleasant place," he added. "There's just something about it I don't really like that much."

"How can you say that?"

How indeed? He swallowed some wine. "We're on an island, really. A creek on both sides. I didn't walk all the way around it. The island is shaped sort of like a bay leaf."

"How wonderful!"

"Or, maybe more exactly, like an eye."

"We'll explore it together when it stops raining."

The thought troubled him. "There isn't that much to look at really. Even the creeks aren't much. No doubt in the summer you can walk across either of them, stepping on the stones."

They slept in front of the fire. It spat and sizzled, then grew quiet as the light from it died. Rain pattered on the roof high above them, and from time to time a tiny cone would fall from one of the redwoods, and roll down the slope of the roof.

This time the dream began like any dream. Paul stood alone in a friendly place. Perhaps he was getting ready to paint, or wallpaper.

He was in a house that had suffered neglect. And only when the steps began did he realize where he was. It was the cabin, and he was in the downstairs bedroom looking at the tape recorder, and he could not move. He could not move his arms, or his legs, and when he tried to call out he could not speak.

14

Paul stirred some oregano into the scrambled eggs. The percolator was chattering, and although he did not care for percolated coffee, he had to admit that it was a jolly sound.

"To be absolutely fair," he continued, "you should bring three friends, and share the food. One fish dish, one of poultry, and one of whatever seems most difficult. It can be fun, but after a while it becomes a little like scouting the minors for players with a major-league curve. You see a lot that are pretty good, but very few that are excellent."

"I thought you like to do it all by yourself."

"Yes, I do. I find the effort to be sociable and eat seriously at the same time to be a strain. So I wind up going three or four times to the same restaurant, ordering something different each time, probing for weakness. I always find it."

"Always?"

"Perfection itself is a fault. The impeccable restaurant is usually sterile. Too quiet. Too pretty. Not enough hearty laughter."

"You're impossible to please."

"No, once you realize you can ruin anybody with a few sentences you realize you have to try to be fair. You have to consider things objectively. What the restaurant offers for the price, for example. How much parking is available. Things like that. I've learned to at least try to be judicious."

He poured coffee into two red porcelain cups. A scum of oil formed on the surface of the coffee, the inevitable result of perking.

Paul had grown to dislike bad coffee, and wondered if bad coffee was better than none at all.

"Did you have a bad dream?" she asked.

Paul scraped the eggs onto the plates. One plate was a fine piece of Spode, the older Spode, when they were still reliable. The other was blue melmac. Paul served the melmac to himself, although the scratched cheapness was disgusting.

"Last night," she continued. "I thought you had a nightmare."

"I don't know," he lied. "I can't remember."

"It sounded pretty frightening."

"Maybe it was. I can't remember."

"I slept very well." She seemed proud of this fact.

The coffee was ghastly. Paul winced, and apologized for bothering to make it. "Better to drink nothing, than drink something that tastes like antifreeze."

Lise left to go for a walk, and Paul found himself hoping that she would not see the graves. He did not understand why, but he wanted to protect her from them.

He washed the dishes feeling meditative, which is how he usually felt when he washed dishes. He rinsed out the sink and dried his hands when he heard the pounding of steps on the front stairs.

Lise was wild-eyed. "The bridge is out!" she gasped.

For a moment, Paul could not move. Then they both ran outside, and down the long slope through the pouring rain. They staggered, panting, and held on to branches to keep from falling.

The creek was the color of milk chocolate. It surged and roiled, uttering a grumbling roar that shook them as they watched. Black stumps pierced the water, and foam swirled around them. It was not easy to see that the bridge was gone, because there was no evidence that there had ever been a bridge, except for the black timbers that punctured the flood.

Paul could not speak. He danced down to the edge of the creek, and the bank collapsed. Water tore at him as he reached for something to grasp. He found something, and squeezed. It was only mud.

For a few moments Paul thought: Don't worry. It'll be fine. But now he saw that it would not be fine. The torrent jammed him against a root, a gnarled, bronze-dark club thrust into the rain. He gripped it with both hands.

He could not pull himself up, and he knew if he let go he would die.

He was drowning.

This can't be water, he thought. It's too strong. He held on to the root, and strained to haul himself from the flood.

"Stay away!" he called to Lise, who skittered near the bank and slipped. She hunched herself away from the creek, calling words Paul could not hear. She held out her hand to him, as though at that distance her hand could help him.

He thought: Drowning.

And then he swung himself out of the flood. He crawled, feeling strangely amphibian, afraid to attempt his feet until he was far away from so much as a puddle.

It rained harder, and Paul let the clean rain wash the mud from his clothes, standing up in it, letting the cleansing drops strip him of mud and leaf rot.

They helped each other through the trees like two frail people. They undressed each other before what remained of a fire, and tossed new logs onto the coals. They drank still-warm coffee, and Paul was thankful for it.

"We're trapped!" he whispered. "There's no way out of here."

They huddled in blankets.

"We'll get out eventually," he continued. "It can't rain forever. Besides, there's no way the water can reach us." He wanted to reassure her, and kept talking. "We're completely safe. We have plenty of food."

She looked at him in a measuring way. "You could have drowned."

"I know it. It was horrible." He thought of it as something that was already in the distant past. "If it hadn't been for that root, I would have drowned."

She put a hand out to him.

"Or, maybe not," he said. "Who knows what might have happened? Another branch, or a rock somewhere." But he had a very distinct image in his mind: his body, pale as chicken fat, crammed into the mud somewhere downstream. It was a particularly ugly image, and very real.

"We'll stay inside, in here where it's safe," she said.

He did not answer.

"What do you know that I don't?" she asked.

"Nothing. I don't know anything."

"What are you hiding?"

"I'm not hiding anything," he said feebly, but he had always known that she was smarter than he was. "I have only suspicions. Doubts."

"About what?"

"About Len."

"We already talked about that."

"There are some graves," he blurted. "I didn't want you to know. I thought you might be afraid."

"Christ." She shook her head. "Why would some graves scare me? We knew he picked a place with something creepy about it. So he could take pictures of ghosts, or whatever."

"You like this."

"I'm not afraid of it. You've been trying to protect yourself, not me. Stop trying to defend me from the horrible. I'm quite capable of facing the world of the spirits without being defended by you."

This was a very harsh rebuke, and Paul felt it deeply. He sulked into the downstairs bedroom, and stared at the tape recorder for a long time. It was an unremarkable room. The only things in it that were of any interest at all were the tripod, with a small camera, and the tape recorder, next to which were some TDK D-C90 cassettes. And the gray metal box.

He wasn't afraid. The real fear of the water surging around him had cleansed him of all imagination. He wrapped the blanket more closely around himself.

"I'm sorry," she said.

He nodded that he was all right.

"It's been a difficult morning. We shouldn't wander around this freezing place dressed in blankets."

"No, we shouldn't," he said, but he did not move.

"Don't keep any more secrets from me," she said.

He knew, then, that he should tell her about the dream. The way it recurred. The way they had all experienced it. Instead, he said, "There is something on these tapes that can help us."

"I expect the tapes are much like his graveyard films."

"Inconclusive?" he asked, borrowing her word.

"Very."

As he warmed himself at the fire he found himself watching the stuffed head of the deer. The hair had worn away from parts of the neck, and bare, leathery hide showed through. The dark hairs on its snout were much like the hairs of a cat. Its ears were as large as a man's hands, and its glass eyes were dark brown; they seemed to stare down into the room.

15

The stones were gray words pressed into a surface as black as a burned field. I could not see them—but if I looked away, toward the totally empty black, they were all around me.

So I have come again. They all knew why I was here. I could sense them inhaling the emptiness around them. Inhaling the dark.

Breathing me.

I was empty. There was nothing left. There was only the Other in me now, that Voice that called me and breathed into me.

I was fading, like someone overexposed. Even in the darkroom film will cloud. Even far away from light. I was blank, now, empty.

I thought: You have not left me alone.

Of course not, He said, His Voice in me like pleasure. You know how much I love you.

Not wanting to say it. And wanting it. That was all that was left of me.

Yes. I know.

Why have you waited so long?

I thought: just a few pictures. Just a few, and then I'll go.

My camera. I clutched it, thankful for it. Ideal for this. Not as ideal as the Hasselblad, but that camera needed a tripod and I did not want to drag a tripod over the walls and into this place. It would slow me down, and they could catch me here.

Oh, Len. I have waited so long.

Just a few pictures. I held my breath. The Leica would see. An M6, with a Summilux lens. My hands trembled. Just a few pictures.

The camera was cold and heavier than usual, because I was weak, all the strength evaporating from me.

Before His strength.

I've waited so long.

Just a few pictures. Then I'll go.

Come and see me Len. Let me love you. Bring the camera. I want everything you want.

Granite is so cold. So perfect, entirely, from its skin, through to its heart. Pressing my forehead against a stone, I could not enter it. I could not plunge into the perfect, other world.

Come to me.

That Voice like a bow across a cello string, a tight, hard string, and I knew He had me, and I wanted Him. I could feel myself tighten, wanting His Voice across me.

Come to me, Len.

He was all that I was not, and his Voice everything I wanted, and yet I trembled. It was too cold, and the camera too heavy, and my arms water clouding into ice.

I ran. The spear-pointed fence burned my hands with its chill, and I fell on the outside, weeping.

Please.

He was begging.

Come back. That Voice like silk across granite. Please.

His voice is me, His perfect strength:

Don't make me wait any more.

16

Paul's aunt, Mary Lewis, watched the performance of *Romeo and Juliet*, admiring as always the healthy young men with their genital bulges, but she could not pay much attention to ballet on this night. Mark, her most recent boyfriend, tugged a well-tailored pant leg and put his two hands together.

He was a handsome man, but all of her men had been handsome, including her husband Phil. Phil had been dead only seven years, but already he seemed, like his rows of books, to belong to the past. A rich and vigorous past, but one that was unattached to the present except as objects of memorable beauty. Phil had been the best-looking, and for a while the most intelligent, of all of them. Shortly after Phil's death she had retaken her maiden name, and lived as though Phil had died long ago, in another age.

The first act ended, and the dancers acknowledged the applause. The orchestra became what orchestras always become when they stop playing, a collection of gawky men and women with a jumble of sheet music, gossiping cheerfully among themselves like so many bus drivers, or substitute teachers.

"You seem restless," said Mark.

"I am, a little."

"Still having trouble sleeping?"

She should not confide so much in Mark. He might become possessive. She put her fingers to her hair, aware that one did not easily discuss one's sleeping habits, even if in a private box.

Still, she must have mentioned it in passing a few days ago. She was a private person, but we all have to share our little anxieties. She would, however, never share her big anxieties. Or perhaps she should call them her big terrors.

She could never discuss them with anyone.

"You ought to visit my doctor. I've told you about him before."

"Often," she smiled, meaning: too often.

"If nothing else he could suggest some pills. I know—you don't take pills. I hate them. But you're wearing yourself out."

This, she knew, was a gentle way of telling her that her nerves were affecting her looks. This was bad news indeed.

"I have an excellent doctor," she began, but she didn't, really. She had a doctor she had known since her Stanford days, a jovial man as careful with his patients as with his horses, and fortunately she had never taxed his command of medicine. She had always been healthy. Never sick. Strong, always.

Physically, at least.

Of that other side of her, of that twisted, animal side—that was what Phil called it—no one knew, except for one person. One frail mortal. The only person she cared about in the world, who was being strangled year by year with what she had done to him.

Discovering what she really was had driven Phil away from her. He had not even tried to save his son, feeling that it was too late.

Her ultimate threat had been that she would go public and tell the press the same lie that she had told her husband. Which, of course, she would never have done. But Phil had returned. Not as a husband, of course. And not even as a healthy man, because the lie had wasted him, and left him a bitter, gray shadow. He had died only a few years later, unable to speak to her, unable to bear her presence. It was as if he had died of hatred.

She naturally wanted anything but publicity. That was why she had asked that nephew to try to find Len, because the young man was smart enough to locate Len, and smart enough to keep quiet about anything disgusting he might uncover. He was also self-absorbed enough that he might never realize the truth at all.

"Really," Mark was saying. "I'm worried about you."

Her looks were suffering. This was a bitter truth.

"Maybe I will," she said with mock weariness, which she hoped disguised the genuine exhaustion she felt. She touched his chin with a coquettish gesture of both affection and disapproval. "If it makes you happy."

The crowd was that interestingly multicolored hive of tasteful and outlandish clothes, furs and silks mingling with peculiar denims she supposed passed for stylish among the unmoneyed. She smiled and nodded at a familiar face, praying that the greeting might not have to flower into speech later in the evening, and then settled back into her chair, hoping that the box rail would shield her from the eyes of what was, after all, society.

"I thought Prokofiev was one of your favorite composers," Mark was saying, manfully attempting to hold idle but intelligent conversation.

"Oh, he is, of course," Mary responded, but why "of course"? And why even bother to respond, when at last the fear she had so successfully buried inside her for so many years was burning inside her like a white-hot splash of lead? "Although I suppose I prefer Mahler."

"I think I do, too." Mark showed his perfect, capped teeth, and she studied his salt-and-pepper handsomeness for a moment.

She had always been lucky in her choice of men, and they had always thought themselves fortunate to have won her attention, if only for an evening. And this was such a successful man, a lawyer by inclination, although not need, an expert on horses and small and very fast cars, the names of which she could never remember. A charming man in every way, as she knew she was charming, bright-eyed and attractive, although her youth was but a distant— painfully distant—flash of diamonds and champagne.

In one sense, though, age would not matter, because she had a reputation for elegance and what that society columnist with a glass eye had called "the magic of knowing exactly what to say." What not to say, she reminded herself. What not to say, even to herself.

But now the nightmares, and Len's disappearance, made the hour a bit late. It was far too late to help herself. She had damned herself to ash, if there were any justice. But perhaps there was still a speck of hope for Len.

She smiled at that thought.

The musicians turned pages of music and quieted into a group of people who could be ignored, except for the sounds which they produced.

"My strong little girl" her father had called her, smelling of leather and cognac and those spicy cigars he had made to his own recipe in London. *Strong* was a word he used more than any other. Instead of saying he felt well, or happy, he would say he felt strong. This desire for, and pleasure in, strength made him survive a fencing accident when she was a girl, an accident which she witnessed, teddy bear in hand, in the brightly lit expanse of the private gym.

The grinning Frenchman had been sweating with the workout her father was giving him when he lunged forward so gracefully he stayed for a moment, out of a desire never to make another less perfect movement again, ignoring the fact that the foil had shattered through a flaw in French metallurgy, and that the point had slipped into the only portion of flesh exposed beneath the fencing mask her father wore, which made his head resemble the gigantic single eye of a fly.

Her father had put a hand to his throat as if only slightly concerned at the sudden scarlet freckles that appeared on his padded chest. His hand, too, became splashed with amazingly bright splotches of crimson, and a long rat's tail of red appeared at her father's throat, then vanished. It appeared again, and only then did Mary understand that her father's life blood was squirting into the resin-scented air.

The Frenchman had turned to Mary, as men had always ever since turned, for help. Wordless, and instantly pale, the Frenchman's English was gone and he gaped at her as if she were to blame for the frailty of steel. She turned away from him, as one turns from savagery, and ran across the green lawn to the telephone.

Her father survived to fence again, with the same Frenchman, perhaps secretly hoping that a foil would snap in a similar fashion, skewering another throat.

There were no more accidents, except for the last, fatal one, her father brought down "like William the Second," her mother had exclaimed. A fellow hunter had discharged his gun, mere birdshot, into the side of her father's head. His head was damaged only slightly, but mortally. It had been, oddly, not a sad event for Mary. Her father had wanted to die in a manly way, and while birdshot was scarcely warlike, she had not seen her father's perfect, embalmed corpse as one that had been insulted.

It was early in the morning when the news came. Her mother had been up since even earlier in the morning, when it was still dark, and although this was not unusual Mary sensed that her mother was in pain.

She rarely spoke to her mother. She loved her, she supposed, but it was the same love she might have had toward a delicate work of art in a distant corner. Her mother's hands always trembled, even when she gathered flowers. There was always a tremor, a vibration, as if life itself hummed too violently for her body.

Her mother was in the study, with the heads of animals she detested, a pale figure under the trophies on the wall. "What's the matter?" said Mary.

"I couldn't sleep," her mother said. Not a complaint. A simple report.

"You should stay up late and get tired."

Her mother smiled wanly, the smile of an adult advised by a fourteen-year-old child. "I stay up past midnight. I read, and I think."

Yes, thinking. Mary knew what her father thought about his wife's "thinking." "Idle brooding," he said. "Sucking on the past like a tick. Absolutely no use to anyone."

"You should run around and get tired."

"Mary," her mother said suddenly. "I had a terrible dream."

Mary did not say, "Father says you dream too much," but she thought it, and her mother sensed the thought. Her mother clutched the robe at her throat and stood. For a brief moment Mary wanted to protect her. "Did you have breakfast?" she asked.

"You know I can hardly stand the thought of food in the morning," her mother said.

"You need your strength," said Mary, repeating a phrase she had heard somewhere, but already she was not interested in whether or not her mother ate.

"In the dream, there was something wrong with your father."

Mary scratched her thigh.

"Your father lay down in the leaves. He looked straight up into the trees, and then suddenly looked straight at me. What a terrible look! I could hardly move! And he grinned, such a ghastly grin."

"What happened?"

"I don't know."

Mary slumped, disappointed. The dark eyes of the moose looked ahead across the room, and seemed to regard her for a moment with a kind of amusement. "That doesn't sound too scary."

"No, I guess it really doesn't. But what woke me up was realizing that it wasn't a dream."

"It's silly," said Mary, and regretted it. Her mother had feelings, after all.

"Yes, it is silly." Her mother laughed gently, and Mary left to have scrambled eggs and cocoa.

The phone rang, and Henrietta answered it, the woman with skin the color of butterscotch, and a gentle New Orleans syrup in her voice. Mary paid little attention, annoyed with the scum that had formed on her chocolate.

Henrietta appeared, however, and put one large hand over Mary's. "You better go in and be with your mother," she said.

"What's wrong?"

Henrietta's eyes looked deep into Mary's, trying to will the knowledge into her. "I think your mother should be the one to tell you," she said.

"It's an accident," said Mary.

"Yes, it's an accident."

Mary wanted to ask more, but she had run out of questions. Accidents involved cars, and everyone she knew drove very well. Her father had run into something, she supposed.

She ran into the study, but the heads of animals looked down into an empty room. She found her mother in a little-used bedroom. Plastic sheets covered the Chippendale, and the frames on the wall held simple etchings, bridges over anonymous rivers, troubadours singing to women who looked away, admiring butterflies.

"There's been an accident," said Mary.

"Close the door," said her mother.

Her mother rarely gave a simple command. Mary closed the door, but kept her back against it.

Her mother held her hands palm-down in her lap, and spoke as if to them. "Something has happened."

Mary felt a flicker of confidence. She had known this much already.

"While they were hunting."

Mary flashed into uncertainty.

"A gun went off—" Her mother stopped and clenched her fists. When her hands had relaxed again, she said, "And your father was hit."

A grinning face, thought Mary. So he can't be in pain.

"They thought he could be helped, but there was nothing the doctors could do."

Mary realized that she was supposed to understand, but she didn't. "A gun went off and Father was in the way?"

"Yes. And the shot hit him, and now he's dead." *Dead* was said as a high, pure note. Her mother wept quietly. Mary touched her, incredulous. Only her mother's grief told her the truth.

She climbed into a plastic-shrouded chair, and listened to the shuddering of her mother's narrow body. Mary had never conceived of such a thing, and was nearly nauseated. When she could move again, she crept from the room, and downstairs, into the study.

The heads of the animals surveyed her, and surveyed the room, and surveyed the chair her father had used, and the row of pipes beside the humidor. All those eyes, gleaming, dark, promising her that her father was powerful. They were proof, these conquered beasts. Her father's might was not diminished.

And when she saw his body she was convinced that he was not really there. His face was too delicate, his nostrils tiny slits, his lashes perfect.

He wore a black wool suit, and a tie of dark blue, in her father's usual Windsor. His hair was impeccably combed, as if her father had just paused before a mirror. The life had been blown from him by magic. He was entire, undamaged. He would smile, and wink and say, "Silly, huh?"

He said nothing.

The fellow hunter was an old drinking friend of her father's, a cardplayer with a red face and hairy hands. He appeared at the funeral white and shrunken, eyes seeing nothing. He looked much more ruined than her father, and although she would see the man from time to time at weddings or other funerals, the man never regained his previous color, and seemed shorter, as if in a moment he had lost his strength, firing not shot but vitality into the unsuspecting skull of his companion, killing him as breath kills a candle.

One evening several days later her mother called her into the study. Mary stepped into the room, then shrank to the wall. The dozens of trusting eyes were gone.

"I couldn't stand to see them," her mother said.

Now Mary wept. Her father's presence had been stripped from the house. She could not despise her mother, although she wanted to. Her mother's voice was thin as she explained, "They reminded me of so much pain. So much unnecessary pain."

Her mother held out her arms to Mary, and they held each other, but Mary felt that her mother had made a mistake. Her father belonged in this house. She knew that he would find a way back.

"We have to learn," her mother said, "to be life-givers, not death-dealers," but her mother's voice was so feeble that Mary sensed it was an impossible task.

Three or four years later she stopped before a diorama in the Natural History Museum in San Francisco. Two deer fed off the branches of a tree. Mule deer, the sign explained, and their large ears, their ebony hooves, were unspeakably beautiful. Hills rose and fell behind them, an oil painting dotted with bushes that looked much the way mesquite looks when it stubbles distant slopes.

And yet, the deer were not real. Stiff, shielded by glass that dimly reflected her blouse and skirt, they stood exactly where they were no matter how often she looked away and then back again. They were an illusion. She had always known this. But she knew it again, and it pleased her.

Her father's trophies had been empty husks, no more animal than a clotheshorse is human. And when they were removed what was taken away amounted to little more than cages over which hides had been stretched. Her father did not need those masks.

She left the museum and strolled into the darkness of the aquarium. Bright tanks of fish pulsed and danced, graceful shapes like hundreds of eyes.

Her father needed nothing. He was waiting somewhere to make his presence felt. Even now, he was waiting for her, or perhaps preparing to return. She believed in him. He would find a way.

In a huge tank at the edge of a corridor, a creature longer than a man leaned against the glass, mashing its bulk against the glass. The air of the corridor stifled, and faces were lit by the light from the habitat of the gigantic beast.

Manatee. It fed on a head of lettuce, and bits of cellulose drifted down in the water, large motes of plant material that clung to the occasional hairs of the creature's sides.

"Yuck!" said a boy.

"I'd hate to look like that," said a girl.

"It doesn't mind," said Mary, although she didn't even know the girl.

"I would," said the voice in semidarkness.

No, you wouldn't, Mary thought, but she did not bother arguing. The manatee's crumpled face and small black eyes were beyond such quibbles. It chewed. The head of lettuce swam out of reach, but the manatee caught it just in time. A leaf detached from the head, and drifted, high above them all, on the quaking surface of the water.

The manatee was at peace. It was beyond even contentment. It knew something Mary could not even guess. It was giant with wisdom. If such a creature trusted the world, she could, too.

And years later, when she was pregnant and felt as huge as the manatee, she trusted more than the world she could see. She trusted the world she could not see.

She trusted her father.

17

Phil had attracted her because he so closely resembled her father, a tanned, Scotch-drinking skier when she first met him, strong and good-humored. Except that he had used too much Scotch in the late evenings, stumbling upstairs the way her father never had, and then had the nerve to blame her for his weakness.

Frigid. He would spit the word, stinking of liquor, and then during the years when he stopped drinking and she had softened— warmed, he said—there was still distance between them, an air of mutual disappointment.

Her son had been her only pleasure, and at first it seemed natural. Of course she declined the services of a nurse, and of course she wanted to have the boy taught at home, because she wanted to be close to him, and even when a series of flustered tutors had left, perplexed and complaining that they had done nothing wrong, Phil had suspected nothing. He understood that Mary was perhaps too fond of the boy, no doubt because he so closely resembled her father. The resemblance was profound. Young Leonard looked like a slim, frail version of his grandfather, and Mary had been ecstatic some- times watching her son run across a lawn. Her father was alive again in the bones and blood of her son. Sometimes she meant it literally, frightened, nearly, that her father's spirit was actually present in the flesh of her boy, but other times she realized that this was merely nature's way of perpetuating the genes of that proud and virile man. Either way, when she was with Leonard, she was with her father.

Phil said he never wanted another woman. He would stroke her, explaining how he needed her in the quiet dark of their bedroom, although she preferred to sleep in a bedroom of her own down the hall, where she ordered a designer every year to do something interesting, something that would make the walls and the floor come alive.

Mary would give in to Phil, understanding his needs, and realizing that although he was an insect compared with her father, he was, in the eyes of the world, a desirable husband. The eyes of the world had always mattered to Mary. To appear cheerful and sophisticated was to earn envy, and envy was power. Power to do what? she asked herself sometimes, because she was not smug, and she was not stupid.

Simple power was enough, its own end. She was a jewel, and her husband and her son were the fine setting. Except that night after night she hungered for the touch of her father, his manly laugh, his rough-gentle hands, the way he had tossed a football to her, so that the ripe leather of it had seemed to breathe under her fingertips as he laughed. "Throw it back! And let's see a spiral."

And she had thrown it back with a spiral, while her mother, that pale spoonful of spit, would watch from the steps, disapproving her daughter's masculine ways, disapproving her father's attention, her father's fondness, the way her father would caress his daughter after a day of riding, his intelligent, strong hands soothing her back as if she were a filly as he told her she was the best horsewoman who had ever lived, and he was proud to have her as his daughter.

The night came when her husband was again drunk, the bottle of twelve-year-old single malt on the floor beside him, his snoring mouth like the mouth of a salmon exhaling the sour stink of a man who does not know how to live his life.

"You are disgusting," she told the rattling carcass. "Weak. Empty. Worthless." The words were weak. She could not enunciate her contempt.

Like an answer, his breath caught and he coughed.

She waited for him to wake, but he did not. She hungered for him to rise for a moment so she could tell him what she thought, but he was beyond that, a man who had transformed himself into a heap of garbage.

She wept, furious that she had to live with such a wasted man. Her father could drink all night, and never waver. He could laugh as heartily at dawn, smoking yet another cigar, as he had laughed the evening before. His card companions would reel apologetically, and he would saunter, in control of every movement, assisting them into their coats.

And then she awoke to the understanding that her father was alive that moment, waiting in that house, to show his contempt for Phil in the best way a man could show contempt for another. Not that her father had ever expressed contempt; such a feeling was too base. But you could see in the glint of his eye that he knew that he was superior to a man who complained too much, or couldn't hold his drink.

She slipped through the house like a wraith, called to where he lay, a proud man in the body of a youth, but calling to her, willing her to him, up the carpeted stairs, the unheard signal of his will drawing her in like a trout on the long, transparent line.

She was in his room, and his eyes were alight. "Father," she whispered. "Take me away from this."

And his eyes glittered, and she understood that her father had felt more than a father's love for his daughter. "I can't," she groaned, kneeling beside the bed. "I can't stand it any more."

She gripped the hand, her father's hand, her son's hand, and held it. She gripped it, squeezed it until it must be agony, but of course there was no cry, and she knelt there beside the bed imagining the walls dissolving as the room soared into the air, the bay, the hills and the distant lights of faraway cities scattering around them, like playthings.

18

Mary asked Mark in, but of course the tone of her asking was deeply asexual, and he thanked her the way a man will when he is about to decline, but he said yes.

To her regret, he wanted Scotch. "I thought you preferred bourbon."

"Usually. But I feel like Scotch tonight."

Sandy, the Filipino slip-of-a-thing, brought them drinks, and vanished in the way that made Mary prize her. "I do prefer a full-length ballet to one of those mix-and-match shows they put together."

Mark seemed to mull this, or savor the Scotch, but it turned out to be neither. "I might as well be straightforward," he said.

Mary drooped inwardly. Men were always tedious when they resolved to be straightforward or honest. But whatever could he have to say? He seemed to be waiting for a nod from her, and when men need permission to speak they are about to say something they are afraid no one wants to hear. She smiled quickly and tilted her head quickly, and then resumed an expression she could wear like a mask, that of bored benevolence.

"I have been considering our future."

"Ah!" Was she surprised? A little? No, not at all. And yet, one is always a little surprised to have one's scantest suspicions leap into fruit.

He was old enough, and calculating enough, to seem calm. But she knew he was nervous. She would make a man nervous, because she struck men as capable of breaking them like sticks. Her next words had to be chosen with care, but could not seem to be the result of much thought. Such words required high craft.

"The future is imaginary," she began, and she knew he would have to feel disappointed. "It is an invention. Not even worth thinking about."

He smiled, an attractive man.

"You knew my husband?"

Calling Phil "her husband" was a signal. But Mark took it well. "Yes. Not well, but we saw each other from time to time and said hello. I always admired him."

"He was a remarkable man. All these books—" The books shifted in the firelight, and a sudden gust spattered rain against the window. "He was a clever man. And he asked me, in the weeks before his death, not to remarry too soon. Not that I was impetuous, or at that time young."

He made a grimace of protest, as she had expected him to. "But it has been years, now," she added. "I can do whatever I want to."

Mark leaned forward, seeing nothing but her, and she wanted to scream, because she would marry him in an instant except for Len. If not for Len anything would be possible, but Len, whose life she had made monstrous, needed her.

"Have you met my son?"

"Yes, at the reception at the Legion of Honor several years ago. A bright young man. Won awards in photography, I understand."

"Yes," she said sadly. She phrased the next words with her highest skill. "But he is a very sick young man. Emotionally disturbed. I think drugs had something to do with it. He has been a burden to me, but I must accept it. Still, I couldn't ask you, Mark, to share in this burden."

"How sick is he?"

"Quite."

"Mary, I am an experienced person. I know what the world is like. I'm willing to take on the shared responsibility for your son."

Of course, Len was sick. Sicker than she wanted to tell Mark, sicker than she wanted even cousin Paul to know. But most of all she didn't want anyone to know what role she had played in twisting

Len into what he was. All she wanted was to have Len safe. Alive. Somewhere.

Mark sensed indecision. He stepped to her side, for the first time that evening, perhaps for the first time in years, wooden and unsure of himself. He kissed her cheek, and she scented Scotch and the starch of his collar. "I'd be good for you," he whispered.

She believed him.

"I suppose we don't really know each other that well," he said.

"I think I know you, and certainly trust you, as a very dear friend."

He smiled again, that acknowledgment of disappointment accepted with grace. "I would like to know you better. Much better. Because every moment I've spent with you has made me hungry for more."

She turned away from such talk. It pleased her, of course. But if he knew her at all well—if he really knew—he would be disgusted.

"I have what you would have to call a contented life," he was saying. "I lend my name to a successful practice. I travel. I listen to music. But at the very center I have sometimes felt my life to be . . . a little bit empty."

She wondered just how experienced he was. Well-seasoned, perhaps. And sure of himself. But had he any idea how evil the world could be? "I don't believe any part of you is empty."

"I am very happy. Make no mistake about that. Emptiness has never bothered me. I enjoy going for walks and listening to Vivaldi. I seem to have the gift of simply avoiding anxiety." He smiled, as if ashamed of himself. "But when I'm with you, I know I am with a human being whose life is full. Much richer, and more exciting than mine. A person who has a center."

"Good heavens."

"I'm sorry. I am being foolish. But why not? I admire you, Mary, a good deal."

It hurt her to hear it. It meant that she should not see him after tonight. It meant that he would be shocked if he knew the truth. "I heard someone say that you have a fine legal mind."

"People say things without thinking."

"No one with a fine legal mind can be altogether empty, can they?"

"You're arguing with me about the state of my soul." He put down his drink. He took her hand and held it in his hands for a moment, and then turned away. "And I can see that I have not said the right things tonight."

She hungered to reassure him, but it was better that he leave, and gradually fade from her life. "I would not dream of arguing about the state of anyone's soul. Souls in general are far out of my field of knowledge." Although this was not, she thought, quite true.

"I enjoyed your company tonight," he said, and it seemed the beginning of a speech of farewell.

More than anything she wanted to beg him not to leave. But she could not involve this decent man. He must go on believing that she was what she seemed to be: a lively, beautiful woman, and nothing more.

"It was a very pleasant evening," she said, and his smile told her that her words hurt him. To her surprise, she was trembling. "I don't know when I have enjoyed the ballet more."

When he was gone, the shadows of the furniture were dark, and shifted back and forth, like living things.

She tilted the glass of his Scotch and gazed into it, the amber liquor blazing with reflected firelight. Then she turned and flung the Scotch into the fireplace. The flames burned white for a moment, and she watched until they died down.

"Would you like a toddy, ma'am?"

"No, I think I'll sleep better tonight."

"I hope so. You need a night's rest."

Mary smiled wanly. Yes, everyone could see it. The secret was wasting her away, just as living with it had wasted Phil.

Just as it was destroying Len.

She laughed, and Sandy turned, startled. "I'm all right, Sandy. Don't worry. I'm sure I'll sleep well tonight. I can feel it deep inside me. There is no question in my mind. Tonight I sleep."

"Len never goes anywhere," Phil had once said. "He never has any friends over. I don't even think he has any friends. Does he?"

She had stopped brushing her hair for a moment. "No. I don't think he does."

"You like that. You like having him to yourself."

"You are being spiteful tonight, Phil. Are you tired of your Latin?"

"You like keeping him as a kind of pet."

"He's not a pet. He's more of a man at seventeen than you'll ever be."

"That poor little worm! He's a pale, skinny little teenager."

She slapped him. "He is twice the man you are. He watches you leave in the morning and his eyes are bright with pity for you, because he sees the kind of worthless coward I'm married to."

Phil held his face where she had struck him, and eyed her. "What both of you need is a kick in the butt."

"You wouldn't dare touch him. He'd tear you limb from limb."

"You're crazy. The poor kid's puny. He's pale from staying in his darkroom all day. He has all the vigor of a slug."

She hit him again before she could think, hard. "He's tougher than anyone you've ever known. Powerful. Capable of taking any kind of punishment without crying out, capable of pleasing me!"

She would never quite decide what lust for brutality had made her tell her lie. The time seemed ripe, and she spoke evenly, slowly, so he would believe her. "He is my lover. He makes love to me while you are asleep, drunk out of your mind. While you are playing with your books he is mounting me, muscular and hard."

It was not, of course, the truth, and she at once regretted saying it, but then strengthened herself. It was the best way to show her spineless sack of a husband how little respect she had for him. It was the best way to hurt him, and he deserved pain for all the lonely, aching evenings she had endured.

"It's not true!"

"It's true! He's mine, all of him, and you have nothing."

She had always been stronger than Phil, emotionally, mentally, in all the ways that mattered. He was weak in the very part of him that should be vital, and he broke and sobbed.

He did not drink himself into a stupor that night. He slowly gathered his suitcases, packed some books, and left; for months afterward she was in terror lest he spread the lie.

Then she was sure that he was the one who was most vulnerable. She had hired a detective and spun Phil back, as a spider reels in the husk of an insect while it is still alive, but paralyzed with poison.

In the last months of Phil's life she had both of them, the spirit of a dead man in a teenager's body, and the spiritless body of a man waiting to die.

He spoke to her about it only once. He had withered over the last few years into a pale scrap, and watched television because he was too weak to read. One day as he sat in the study, unopened volume of Hesiod in his lap, he looked up at her and said, simply, "The worst will happen to you."

"I don't believe in Hell, my dear," she said lightly.

He actually smiled. It was little more than a twitch. "You will find the secret eating you rotten."

"Good heavens, Phil. What a ghastly image."

"And there won't be anything you can do."

"Be quiet, Phil. Nobody knows what is going to happen to anyone."

It seemed as if she had enjoyed the last word. Phil was quiet, and after a while was very quiet and they buried him. It was not the most happy victory in the world, because, although she would never have told him, she had admired Phil's love for books, and the fact that he cared enough for his son to let his horror of his son—and his wife—destroy him.

Her new position as a widow had its charm, and she accepted the clucks of sympathy and the dignified flirtation of eligible money with a good grace. And she was beginning to round into the sort of person who, if she did not have everything, had learned to genuinely dislike what she did not have.

And then Len became very strange.

19

There had been something of the night about him from the beginning, the way he would lie awake with wide eyes, and look into her eyes when she asked, "What's the matter? Can't you sleep?"

"I can sleep if I want to," he would answer, or "Don't worry about me, Mother." His voice too solemn, his tone too aware of things a child should not even guess. From the very beginning she had sensed her father in him. The way he watched her, mocking her with the lift of an eyebrow. The way, if she was upset, he would say, "You mustn't let these things bother you."

"Come and see what I have found," he said one evening in that careful, low voice.

Immediately she did not want to know what this seven-year-old had discovered. And immediately she wanted to: more than anything she had ever desired.

But she did not move. "I'm reading now," she said. "Can't you bring it to me?"

"I'd rather not."

"Is it too heavy?"

He smiled, humoring her. "No, it's not too heavy."

"It's too . . . delicate," she guessed, trying to treat him as if he were an ordinary child, someone who was at heart playful.

He cocked his head. "Why, yes, in a way. It is very delicate. In a way."

"I suppose I'll just have to come look."

He led her down the hall, held the door for her in a well-mannered way, then shut it tight and smiled knowingly, in a way that made her step back and put her hand out to the television set for strength.

"Don't be afraid," he murmured. "It's nothing that will hurt you." He emphasized *you*.

"I must say you have my full curiosity," she said with a laugh. "Whatever could it be?"

He opened the closet door. "I keep it in darkness. Not complete darkness, of course, but then darkness is really almost never complete. There is always a little bit of light if you wait long enough to see it."

"You don't expect me to go in there."

He gazed at her seriously, one hand on the door. "That would be best."

"Bring it out here."

"To bring it into this much light would be agony for it."

"Agony?" He had used the word easily.

"Great pain," he said.

"This is a dim room. The curtains are drawn. You could scarcely read. I don't think that whatever it is would experience agony. At any rate, you'll have to bring it out; I'm not going to—."

He waved her silent, and vanished into the closet. He stepped out of the dark place with a glittering jar, which he placed gently on his desk. He studied the jar with an expression she could not read. When she stepped forward he put a finger to his lips. "Wait," he whispered.

He fumbled into the closet, and withdrew a paper cup covered with a paper lid which a rubber band held in place. He gave her the paper cup without speaking, and to her horror something fluttered within it, like the beating of a tiny heart.

"Look," he whispered.

The jar was empty. A cylinder of glass, a dull gleam where it reflected the line of the curtains. Except, as she studied it, she saw that it was not entirely empty. A crack ran down the side of the glass, a crooked finger of darkness that was not, she saw, stepping closer, a crack at all.

A long skeletal forefinger pointed downward, sealed like a relic in the churches of Italy, a holy digit aged to the point of timelessness. Such things had a certain purity. They were certainly harmless.

She stepped closer, the fluttering thing in her fingers quiet for a moment. It was not a finger. It was a twig. A crook of wood, sealed as if in a vacuum, a relic of earth. It seemed to radiate silence, and she did not want to move lest she disturb something that should be allowed to sleep.

Her eyes were adjusting to the bad light of the room, and she realized that the twig was not alone in the jar. A span of gauze surrounded it like an aura, stretching sloppily from one side of the glass cylinder to the other. It was as if the twig had been used to capture cotton candy, but only a little bit, a few filaments. The pale tissue caught the light from the slit in the curtains, and glowed, like breath on a window.

Len lowered his hand to the lid of the jar, and touched it. He watched the twig for a long time. They would never move again, either of them. They would stand like this until dust covered them, and nothing that happened in the world would reach them.

The fluttering in the paper cup started and stopped.

Something moved in the jar.

A glittering black eye lowered itself from the twig on nothing, and paused. Legs stretched themselves out from the bunched body. The thing waited, listening to them breathe.

There was no doubt in her mind: It was watching them, in the agony Len had described. It was listening to them, to their lungs and their nostrils, but also to all their organs as they worked. The thing in the jar took them in, and waited.

Len held a hand toward her, and she could not move. His fingers twitched impatiently. She gave him the paper cup, and he held it to his ear, his lips parted.

With a metallic chuckle the lid of the jar unscrewed. He held the metal disc above the jar, and then gently found a place for it on the desk. He snapped the rubber band free of the paper cup, and in an instant the paper was off and he held his hand over the container.

The moth fell. The white body with gray wings flew, going nowhere. It stopped, then struggled again, shifting lower in the jar. It dangled, and was free.

And not free, as quickly, as one strand gripped the creature, and it fought, wrestling, wings fluttering, a loud thrumming that echoed in the glass. The glass resounded with it, chiming with it, a brilliant note in the dim light of the room.

The gleaming black eye with elegant legs eased across the gauze. It poised over the white and gray body and, imperceptibly moving its legs, was on it, legs wrapping it, body eclipsing it.

Nothing moved for a long time.

The black legs felt upward, and touched the twig, finding a place on it to rest. The white cylinder in the filaments shivered, and then did not move at all, held frozen in the air like a thing that had no weight.

The lid clattered, and Len screwed it tight. "It's not dead," he whispered.

"No?" she heard herself ask.

"No." He studied the jar for a moment. "No, it's only asleep. The fluid has been injected so that it might go to sleep. It's asleep, now, and it will keep a long time, until the time has come."

She said nothing.

"And when the time has come," he continued, "it will be as fresh as if it were still fluttering around outside. Fresh, and new. And then, after it has been sucked empty, it will keep forever, a perfect specimen that nothing can damage in any way. Because the fluid saves what it destroys."

She forced herself to lay a hand on his shoulder. "This is fascinating," she began.

"I knew you would like it," he whispered. "I knew you would think it was wonderful."

"You have done some reading," she murmured.

"I have read all about them. I know everything about them, and about all kinds of other things, too."

"Don't you wonder if, in some way, it might be dangerous to have such a thing?"

He drew away from her. "It's not dangerous."

"It could be, though, don't you think?"

He smiled at her indulgently, in a way that froze her. "I wouldn't worry about that."

"I only want to protect you from being hurt."

His eyes searched hers. "No you don't. You're afraid."

She could not speak.

"You think you are like the victim. You think you will be captured like that, and put to sleep. But I think I am like the hunter."

"It's a beautiful creature."

"It hates light. It wants to be deep inside things, where it can wait without eating for a long time. When we are in the house, talking and moving around, it can hear us. It hears everything."

"But it doesn't understand."

"We don't know what it understands."

"Of course it doesn't. We are people. We have words. An animal that small doesn't even know about words."

"It doesn't need words."

The black abdomen shrank to the top of the jar, and was invisible.

Mary did not know what to do. She could not bring herself to touch the jar, much less empty its contents anywhere. And she did not want to betray Len. Certainly all boys were interested in things like that. Perhaps he would be a biologist.

Weeks went by, and every night she knew the creature in the jar was listening to every move she made. She knew that Len spoke to it, confiding things to it, and when she saw Len lurking at a screen, glass in hand, she said nothing.

One day Len stopped her on the stairs. "I want to show you something," he said.

"Really?" she said with brittle cheer.

She followed him into his bedroom. The jar was already on the desk. Without speaking he unscrewed the lid, and turned the jar over.

Mary gasped. A black, shriveled thing rolled across the desk. It lay still, a tiny black hand.

The jar was decorated with moths, several of them suspended in mid-jar. Each one was, as Len had said, perfect. It was the beginning of an impeccable collection.

"This was bound to happen," she said.

"I don't see why."

"It was just going to happen. Eventually, it always does."

"I gave it everything it needed."

"Of course you did. And I'm sure it was happy."

"Naturally I knew that someday this would happen. I am not so ignorant. But I thought it would be years from now. It was so safe here. So secluded. Nothing could hurt it."

She touched his hand.

"Now its victims are more perfect than it is."

She expected tears, but there were none. His voice was hard. "You can find another one," she said.

"No. I don't want another one."

Relieved, she picked up the jar. The bodies quaked in the web. "We might as well dispose of these."

"Whatever you want."

"And perhaps you would take the remains and put them outside?"

"It doesn't matter to me. I thought it was perfect."

"Nothing is perfect."

He did not answer. He folded the crumpled thing into a piece of paper. "I'll burn it," he said.

"That's a good idea."

"It always wanted to be invisible, so I will make it invisible."

"Good."

"It told me that darkness was better than light. That light just showed the surface of things, but when it was dark you could see what was really there."

He stared at the folded paper in his hand. "It knew all kinds of things it had just begun to tell me."

On one of those cool San Francisco evenings, as she sat before a fire arranging roses in a vase, he slipped to her side. "It's all right," he said, trembling.

"What's all right?" she said, tilting back from the flowers for a better view.

"I can still hear it."

"Hear what?"

"The hunter."

Her hand stopped. It drew back slowly from the yellow bud and sank into her lap. "You can?"

"It's very distant, and very far away. But I can hear it if I listen very carefully."

She tried to smile. "Whatever does he say?"

"He says he was never really in the jar."

"He does?"

"He says he was somewhere else, and wants me to find him."

"Of course, you burned him up."

"That wasn't really him. He says he's waiting for me somewhere else."

"Oh, really?"

The boy was trembling with excitement. "You don't believe me."

"What does he sound like?" she asked, turning back to her flowers.

"He sounds like this," he said. "'Len. Len. Listen to me.'"

Mary's arms were ice. She groped for the pruning shears to have something solid at her touch. The flowers blurred and faded. The fire was gray, without color.

The boy had spoken in the voice of his grandfather.

20

Even Mary had understood that, in a real way, the spirit of her father did not live inside her son. At least, not every hour. She almost understood that it was only at night, and only in her imagination that this was so.

"Your grandfather is in you," she would tell him, when she began to see it as a strength. "His powerful spirit is in you, driving you like a powerful engine." She gradually wanted it to be true.

Len spoke rarely. Even she noted his profound silence, like a young man listening to commands no one else could hear. But one night she told him about his grandfather's spirit and how it lived inside him, and he said, "I feel it. When you come to talk to me in the night, I feel him enter me as you step into the room."

Except that the next night she felt the soundless call even more powerfully, and entering the room heard him whisper in a voice so like her father's she could not breathe, "Mary!"

She would watch the young man take one of his father's books and sit under a tree, and she would not know anymore what was real. She did not know what she imagined, and what Len imagined. She did not know what powers existed in the house, and in the trees. The city clanged and hummed around them, while in the yard, the secret garden, her son took photographs of birds, and flowers, and studied with tutors she learned to tolerate. The tutors, however, did not enjoy Len's company.

"Are you trying to tell me that my son is not intelligent?" she asked one prim young woman.

"No, I'm not. What I am saying is that it's impossible to tell."

"He is obviously gifted. He built his own darkroom. His photographs are remarkable."

"Yes," said the young woman, with some impatience. "But he never speaks. He never writes. I suppose he can read, and that he has coherent thoughts. But I can't help him if he never expresses himself."

The young woman hesitated, and then added, "He seems to ask about death more than is usual. He asks what it feels like to die. What the dead think about."

"I certainly wonder what it's like. Don't you?"

Another hesitation. "From time to time."

"Sandy, would you please ask Len to meet us here in the garden."

There was a long silence, while the young woman examined her fingernails, which were badly bitten.

Len appeared soundlessly.

"This young woman tells me that you have trouble expressing yourself."

Len was only a few years younger than his tutor. He was a serious-looking young man with dark hair and pale skin. "I have no trouble," he said simply.

Mary thought that the interview was finished, but she added, "You must try to be cooperative with these tutors. They are here to help you."

Len bowed slightly, an odd formality making him seem, in a strange way, very old. He turned to the young woman and was suddenly charming. "You must forgive me if I seemed uncooperative. I have so many things on my mind."

"Of course," the tutor responded, but she never came back.

Len went to a college specializing in people who were taciturn but talented, and won awards for photographs of trees in minimal lighting, so that magnolias in the light of a fragment moon took on the look of a nervous system.

He continued to live at home, but he changed, she could not say exactly when, or how. Gradually she could not see her father in him, but she saw something else. She could not understand what, but she

110

was filled with a hunger to comprehend what she felt she had created.

"Where do you go?" she would ask.

A brief smile as he disengaged a wedge of grapefruit. "I take pictures."

"You didn't come in until three last night."

"I'm an adult." Said not petulantly, but simply.

She tried to keep silent, but found herself speaking. "I worry about you. You never see anyone else. What will happen if I—" She hesitated. "Die."

She had intended to say "remarry," although she had no one in particular in mind.

He looked up at her, and into her, then looked away. "Don't be afraid," he said.

"Afraid of what?"

"Don't be afraid of me."

She began to say that she was not afraid of him, but she stopped herself.

She was.

Every night he would leave just after sunset, and while she knew that many young men went out at night to drink or have sexual liaisons, male or female, she didn't care which, she sensed that he had tasks to perform. He took complicated photographic equipment, tripods and metal tubes of film that dangled from a belt like ammunition.

Most of his pictures he displayed openly in his tidy room. Trees, of course. How she came to despise the enigmatic profiles of trees. Eucalyptus, like tall, pale bones. Redwoods, like the fine-boned skeletons of fish. Poplars, leafless, delicate and anatomical, causing a twinge somewhere inside her body.

All taken in light so scant the judges of contests were amazed at their clarity, and he was asked to write a small book on light-gathering, a technical screed regarding lenses and wavelengths. She read it in secret, praying that it might disclose something about his thoughts, but it was a professional monograph, difficult to follow.

There were two metal boxes, however, which held small prints that she believed were the key to his interests. To his obsessions.

One was unlocked, but she was afraid to look inside it. She was terrified what the photographs might disclose. The other was locked. A simple gray metal box, with a handle.

She asked him once, "Why don't you do anything with the photos you keep in the metal boxes?"

He stared at her.

"They might be interesting, too."

His pale face studied hers. He said, in a whisper, "Don't you ever touch those boxes."

It was not the whisper of her son.

Yet he must have wanted to tempt her, because he did not hide the boxes, or buy a safe that she could not in any way open. He left them in his room, beside a pile of photography magazines, and one day she spied the key to the locked box dangling from a pin on his bulletin board, and found another identical key in his desk drawer among paperclips, attached to a tag marked *Dup.*

As if he were inviting her to look. As if he wanted her, perhaps not quite consciously, to see what the boxes contained.

Sandy, who remarked on almost nothing, said once, "Young Mr. Lewis spends a lot of time out at night." Setting the coffee service on the table, not meeting her employer's eye. And eager to talk to someone, anyone, about her son, Mary had said, "Yes, he is a very mysterious young man, isn't he?"

Sandy, as usual, said nothing, so Mary chattered on. "And I must admit that I wonder where on earth he spends his time." Thinking that perhaps Sandy had glanced into the box on her way from room to room with her ostrich-feather duster.

"I made some sugar cookies," said Sandy.

"Oh, delightful," said Mary. Then, quickly, "I wonder if he has a lover somewhere."

Sandy slipped out of the room, and the plate of sugar cookies was both a confession of ignorance and a rebuke. The cookies were delicate, cut in shapes of quarter moons. "They are delicious," said Mary, eating only one corner of one moon. Of course Sandy would deliberately know nothing. She was proud of her discretion. And of course Mary would never forgive her for it.

The night came when Mary steeled herself to go into Len's room and open the boxes.

She stopped him at the door of the study, the only room in the house where she still felt comfortable. He carried the usual photographic equipment, and barely glanced at her on his way past, and then she touched his sleeve with a finger. "Will you be late?" For once she wanted him to say yes.

"Probably," he said.

"Shall Sandy leave something for you?"

"It doesn't matter."

He turned, but turned back again to look at her, almost seeing that she was going to look inside the boxes on this night. But he said, "Why are you reading that book?" in that electric whisper.

For a moment, she could not speak. It was the leather-bound Ovid, the one Phil had enjoyed more than all his thousands of books. But she could not read Latin.

"I wasn't reading it. I was enjoying it. It's a beautiful volume."

He recognized weakness in her, if not a lie. "Beautiful, but empty."

"Perhaps," she faltered.

"And what is good in it you would not understand."

"Would you?"

"Yes." That whisper. "'I bend close to tell of things that change, new being out of old.'"

She was icy. "Phil admired Ovid, he—"

Len laughed, quietly. "I will be late."

She watched the shine of sunlight off the waxed wood of the floor, afternoon light, gentle and in harmony with every peaceful thing she had ever known, but she could not move. She was ice.

The gap in the row of books attracted her, and she slipped the book into it wishing for the first time in a long while that Phil were alive. She wanted to talk to someone so badly she ached.

"Len, Len," she sobbed. Her Leonard. Her healthy, handsome boy had grown into a creature with the eyes of a dead man.

But all this was her own imagination. She tried to calm herself. She was the one who was peculiar; she had always known that. Whatever Len was, she had made him. She would redecorate. Bring in more flowers, great lances of gladiolus to give fire to the various dark corners of the house. She would have an aviary built and collect canaries. She craved the mindless jabber of birds. They were lively. They had no choice.

She would change everything. She would even take down the Patinir, the one Phil had admired. The translucent angel paused in the air before the shepherd, and she despised the lie. Whatever appears, conjured out of the thin afternoon air, is not an angel.

She paced the garden. She would rip out the roses. How much they reminded her of the truth: beauty with teeth. Her father—now she could barely think of him—had despised roses. "Flowers for women," he had said. He liked clean-lined irises, lupines, phallic bursts out of the masculine earth.

She wept, and then she was strong. It was nearly dark, and she went into the house. When night was everywhere, and not even a dim glow of daylight was left, she went upstairs, turning on lights as she went, and stood before her son's room.

The door was locked. A bright new dead-bolt gleamed at her.

She laughed. She was terrified of Len, but she was not weak. Sandy puttered somewhere in the kitchen, and would not see or hear anything Mary did. Mary was glad there was a lock on the door. It made her cruel.

She dismissed destroying the door with an ax, even if she could find one somewhere in the gardener's shed. She would be crisp. Precise.

She called a locksmith, promising tremendous rewards for lightning service. A small man with freckles arrived panting, swore once or twice beneath his breath, and said he would have to damage the door.

"Damage the door, and I'll kill you," she said calmly.

The locksmith laughed, because of course it was a joke. "Very few men know how to pick a lock like this. It is a very good piece of equipment. Most men would have to drill, and wreck the lock." He worked as he spoke, making a grimace of effort as he fit a long strip of metal into the slot. "Which is the quickest method. This method is difficult."

Scarcely a method at all, she thought, but she remained silent. She even turned away, seething but outwardly calm, as the smell of sweat rose from the man and reached out across the hall.

She paid him extravagantly, as she had promised. The lock turned in her fingers, and the room was hers.

She did not enter for a while. She let herself feel quiet inside. Then she turned on the light, and shut the door behind her, propping a chair under the doorknob. If he returned and saw her here she could not guess what would happen.

The first box, the one that was never locked, was cold in her hands. She lifted it and was surprised that it was so heavy. She hesitated, hating herself for her cowardice, and opened the lid.

A file, with folders and tabs without any writing, blank tabs, as if there were no need for labels. In each folder nestled a series of photographs. Again she hesitated, but she forced herself to open a folder and leaf through the pictures.

She was relieved. More night pictures, most of them not very well done, she thought, certainly moodless. Murky, meaningless pictures. Early work of his, experiments, perhaps. Here she discerned a sidewalk, there a dark bulk of bush. Until, with growing horror, she crept her way through the file realizing that all the photographs were of cemeteries. Crypts, headstones, and interior shots of mausoleums done in very minimal light, at night, in secret.

Morbid, she thought to herself. Very. And yet, what had she expected? Pictures of naked women? Or, even, naked little boys? Of course not. She had understood that her son was a very peculiar person. Why shouldn't he take photograph after photograph of cemeteries? Civilian cemeteries, military cemeteries, some displayed rather well, she thought, admiring a recently filled grave beneath the branches of, she decided, a cypress.

She would encourage him to bring these pictures into the study. They would discuss their artistic merits. There was probably a market for, say, a book of arty shots of graveyards. People found such places romantic, even peaceful. Most of these pictures were beneath his usual quality, but perhaps he was deliberately using sloppy technique, gathering information on cemeteries so he could return again and take even more pictures.

Certainly nothing very impressive here, she sniffed. Almost relieved, she tucked the files back into the box, and was careful to see that they were undisturbed in appearance.

But she was trembling. Her hands were cold.

The locked box awaited her attention.

She had seen enough. She had the general idea of what Len's nighttime interests were; she did not have to see any more.

There was a sound in the hall and she froze. She could not breathe. When she realized that she was mistaken, she was weak. She found a chair and sat, breathing hard. She could not bear to look at the locked box. It was identical to the other one. Gray metal, with a chrome-colored handle, except that it was defended by a small padlock. A flimsy lock, really.

But enough to keep anyone from looking into the box. Enough to make her hands wet and make her legs too weak to move. Enough to mock her, a challenge, a way of telling her that she had made her son into a terrible thing.

She guessed what was in the box. She could not believe it, but so many times in her life she was unsurprised at the supposedly unexpected. She collected her strength. She made herself calm. And she opened the desk drawer and removed the key, a little slip of steel with notches in it.

The padlock fell open, and she detached it. She opened the box. There were more files, nameless manila tabs, but not as many. They leaned back upon themselves as if to avoid her hands.

She slipped one free of the box and paused for a moment before letting it fall open.

Pictures of a crypt. The pale marble of a tomb in moonlight. The tomb bore the name: Lewis.

She closed the folder, trembling so badly she nearly dropped it. She had long ago stopped visiting her father's tomb, although it was a handsome one. To be reminded of his physical presence above ground in a steel box was ugly. She controlled herself, going numb, and slowly, deliberately, took out each folder and looked at each picture, her body growing rigid with horror.

Then, barely able to see, she slipped the folders back into the box, and locked it. She shuddered but she gripped herself, digging her nails into her flesh. When she stopped shuddering she put the boxes where she had found them, moving very slowly.

She took the chair from beneath the doorknob, but she did not bother to shut the door behind her. She did not bother to establish any pretense. Her face was frozen into what she knew must be a grimace, a mask of terror mastered by the most powerful will.

She took each step slowly, and passed by the study. She stepped across the dew-wet lawn in the darkest part of the garden.

She fell onto the grass and sobbed, shuddering, retching, blind with everything she had seen and wishing she had never had eyes, never lived beyond her childhood so she could never have been brought to this.

She hid her face in the damp lawn and groaned into it, and even when she was empty, belly and soul, she still could not move, but lay like a lifeless thing.

21

"You'll have to go. You can't live here anymore."

Len met her eyes. "Why?" he whispered.

"You know why," she said quietly.

For a long moment she thought he might strike her. But at last he laughed, a dry, empty, hissing laugh. He bowed, a quick jerk of his head. "I understand," he said. Why did he seem amused?

For the next few years she had seen less and less of him, although she called him on the phone, hating the sound of his voice, which became almost entirely a whisper, like the sound of something dragged across snow. And he called her once a week, always polite, always secretive.

He went north at last to do "research," as he put it. And then she stopped hearing from him, and what was she supposed to do? She wanted to forget him completely, but that was impossible.

And then the nightmares had begun, the terrible dreams of the intruder in the seemingly peaceful place, the slow steps, and the terror that woke her night after night.

The terror that still kept her awake. She sat in her dressing gown. Rain pattered on the window, and she nearly prayed aloud for sleep. As if she could pray. As if she would be heard even if she did.

She would not be able to sleep. She probably should see Mark's doctor. Sleeping pills would be a blessing, although she wondered if she might take the entire bottle, every single pill, and sleep forever.

The idea was almost amusing. Not that she would ever do that. No, she was not destructive to herself. Only to the people entrusted to her. She ate them like a vulture. She had not wanted to be evil.

It had been tricked into her somehow, at some point. Some alloy in her makeup, the sort of fault that had made the foil snap and turn into a jagged rapier.

Sandy opened the door into the kitchen, spilling light across the floor. "Oh!" she gasped. "It's you!"

"I thought I'd have a toddy, after all. I didn't mean to scare you."

Sandy took over the filling of the kettle. "Tonight, I don't know why. But tonight I am so nervous."

"There's no reason to be nervous," said Mary.

"No reason! Every day all these ghastly things happen. Crazy men all over, hurting people. And always crazy men, you notice. Never women."

"There are sick women."

Sandy paused, bottle of rum in her hands. "Of course. Many miserable women. But they don't go around hurting people. Strangling. Beating to death. Slaughtering innocent people in their houses. Men do that. Crazy men."

Sandy added honey to the cup, and poured rum, the gurgling of the liquor like a sinister chuckle. The sound of it dazed Mary, and she gripped the counter top to bring herself back into what she supposed was reality: the gleaming stove, the faucet a hook that dripped water.

"Men who have no idea what it is to be a human being," Sandy continued. "Who are totally wrapped up in their own minds. Who think the world is all inside their heads." She stirred hot water into the cup. The spoon jangled in the china, and a drop of rum glistened on the countertop. "They should do something about these men."

"What?" Mary whispered. "What can they do?"

"Sometimes I think it would be better for everyone if they did not have news about craziness. If when someone was killed, they didn't even talk about it. How many times have I turned on the television and seen policemen carrying a bag with a body in it."

Sandy was obviously nervous tonight. She was rarely so talkative. "Make a toddy for yourself," Mary suggested.

"No. I will sleep well. Nothing interrupts my sleep. It's just something about tonight. Made me scared."

"The weather."

"I like rain. Comforts me, makes me glad to be indoors. But do you know what? If they didn't have the bad news on television, they'd never catch the crazy men who do all these things."

"Naturally, if something happens, they have to tell us. No matter how ghastly it might be. It is, I suppose, their responsibility."

"That's right. They have to do it. They have to tell us the truth, even if we don't want to hear it."

The drink was still too hot. "We should," said Mary weakly, "try to think of pleasant things."

Sandy nodded. "We will."

Mary turned on the television in her bedroom. Hills and trees, and a herd of wild beasts sprang into focus. A lioness lowered herself into tall, brown grass. The herd twitched. One of the animals was aware of something. Another lioness hulked through the grass.

Her father had hunted in Africa many times, although he had rarely talked about it. What he had enjoyed there was a secret, a ripeness that he had held to himself. Once, squeezing a tick out of a dog's fur, he had remarked that in Africa they had ticks as big as nickels.

The herd churned, and Mary turned off the television. She knew too much about hunters and their quarry.

Someone answered immediately, but she knew it was a switchboard designed more to screen than to admit as soon as she heard the tone of her voice. "I'm sorry, Dr. Kirby doesn't have night duty."

It was important.

"I can have you speak with the physician on duty."

When would Dr. Kirby be in?

"We don't expect him tomorrow, but we do expect him . . ."

Mary could, she supposed, insist on speaking to Kirby. She could identify herself, describe herself as a client, and insist on his home phone. But what could she say? How could she start from the beginning over the phone?

"Is there a message?" the voice was saying.

She had been obsessed with her father, and so broken by his death that she had imagined—or had she believed—that his spirit was alive in the body of her son. That burden had twisted her son into an inhuman thing. But Mary could not say any of this to the bland voice on the switchboard. "No, no message."

"Can I tell him who called?"

Mary smiled to herself. Tell him that a woman who wishes she could change everything she ever did called up and wanted to say hi.

"No," said Mary. "No message."

Mary slept, waking briefly once as rain clawed the window. She listened for a moment to the rain, and then, once again, she slept.

This time the dream was more detailed than it had ever been. The house was dark, and cold, but somehow pleasant, a large fireplace before her with a half-charred log. There was a kitchen off to her left somewhere. She sensed it, and felt that something cheerful was possible there, perhaps even some sauce simmering on the stove. It was raining, but she was safe from the rain.

Then there was a bump upstairs. Someone was treading the floorboards above her, a slow, jerky step. The steps half-stumbled to a doorway, and then someone stood above her, watching her, someone who knew her, and she could not turn around. Whoever it was walked slowly, gathering strength, to the head of the stairs, and once again stood watching her as the rain fell outside.

The person descended the stairs, carefully, the steps creaking with the weight of the body, and when his foot left the bottom step she wanted to turn, she wanted to cry out, but she could not, and then she wanted to wake, but she could not. The steps one after another crossed the floor, a slow, heavy stride that was in no hurry and yet determined, and then the person was just behind her, a long, cold breath on the back of her neck.

A hand fell upon her shoulder and gripped her hard, so hard she wanted to cry out, but she could not. Her voice leaked a long hiss of air, and then she turned her head.

"Len!" she gasped, because it was Len, but then he turned his head so the light fell on it clearly, and it was the ruined face of her father's corpse.

22

She got out of bed at once. She hurried into clothes, barely stopping to decide what to wear with what, because this had not been an ordinary dream.

This had been a warning. Paul should have called by now, and she knew he was in danger.

She had blundered badly by sending Paul into the wine country. She remembered him as a boy, brought over by her husband's sister, a bland woman with a large face. She did not want to cause him any pain, and what was waiting for him in the wine country was worse than pain.

She nearly wept with anxiety as she fastened snaps, and glanced at her face in the mirror. She had aged terribly. Perhaps, someday, after a long voyage among the Greek islands, and long walks along Aegean shores, she would regain her beauty. But now she was shattered, and anyone who saw her would see a broken woman.

She would muster her powers as best she could.

She drove through the early-morning rain. Water spurted from around manhole covers like long, gray tentacles, and lapped over the curb carrying rolls of half-dissolved newspaper.

To her annoyance the locksmith was not familiar to her, a surly Hispanic who seemed reluctant to speak English. She explained that she was an artist who had lost the key to her studio. Dropped it down a street drain, wasn't that the most annoying thing?

He listened to her as if she were a talking tree, and glanced to the Mercedes, parked with one wheel on the curb. He hefted his toolbox, as if the clank of tools communicated something to him.

"It's terrible when a person loses something," she said, "it disrupts not only your life, but your peace of mind, too. And that is so important."

The door was open in five seconds. The locksmith shook his head. "Is no good."

"What?" she said, fumbling for money.

"No good. The lock. I have made it so that now it will no longer work without repair."

"That's all right."

"I will go to my truck and bring another lock."

"It's all right."

"These things happen. It is unfortunate."

"I don't mind. Please don't mention it." She squeezed past him on the stairs.

"There will be no charge. This is a very nice lock. Very well built. It is very unfortunate that I have broken it."

She looked back at him. She calmed herself in an instant. "Yes," she said. "I would very much appreciate it if you would replace it at once. I keep valuable things here." She stared across the expanse of empty floor to the huddle of furniture. "Computers. Cameras. I need a good lock. A lock that will work."

The man knelt to the key slot, and spoke as if into it. "I will fix it."

He lumbered down the stairs, and she scurried to the small living area. Paul had left a very un-Len-like clutter. Canceled checks were scattered across the desk. They were scraped into the most casual semblance of order, and she despaired for a moment that she would be able to follow Paul's tracks, thoughtless ramble that they no doubt were.

She stared into the screen of the computer, finding the distended reflection of her face somehow calming. She let herself grow peaceful, and began to search in her thoughts not for where the hiding place of Len might be, or how she could find out where the name of the place might be hidden, but how Paul might have discovered it.

"I will have it fixed in almost no time at all," called the echoing voice. "It will be a very easy matter."

She nodded, pretending to be impatient, but actually glad to have someone there with her. This place was too cavernous, and too cold. Looking around the room, she felt that Len had never expected to return here. He had taken most of the books he would want to have by his side, and he had put the cemetery pictures into a kind of snapshot album. Tears filled her eyes as she saw the careful, fastidious manner in which her son pursued his madness.

She had told Paul that he was a ghost investigator. She had to offer some explanation for what Paul would no doubt realize was an odd hobby. She wished that he were a ghost investigator. It seemed like such a sane pursuit.

The metal box, the one he had kept locked, was gone. For an instant she thought that perhaps he had changed. Perhaps he had outgrown that obsession. But she laughed at herself. He had simply taken it with him. He would not let himself be parted from such an important collection.

If there were any sign of a memo, a notepad, a letter—anything—Paul had taken it. She was lost. She sat on the bed and stared at her hands. There was nothing she could do. Paul would be destroyed.

She wept. She would not allow herself to collapse. Not now. She dried her eyes with the linen handkerchief her mother had used, one of many her mother had brought back from Italy one spring. Her poor mother. Lost in the shuffle between a sportsman and his daughter, she had simply sat one morning a few months after her husband's death, closed her eyes and died. A stroke, but in the sense of a "stroke of fortune." She had suffered mostly bewilderment in living, and in her death had suffered not at all.

She put her hand on it before she realized what it was. The canceled check read, "North Coast Realty. Deposit, Parker Cabin."

So it would be easy, after all.

"It is fixed now. It is okay."

She put down the phone. Money crackled in her hand. "Thank you."

"No problem," he said, and for a moment seemed friendly. He opened his hand and gestured upward. "This is a big place. A very big place."

"Yes," she said cheerfully, enjoying the obvious. "Yes, it certainly is."

"You are an artist."

"Yes. An artist."

"I am, too."

"Oh?"

"I paint."

"Ah."

But she saw him glancing into the living space, so she added, "I am a photographer, actually. Not quite a painter."

"Photography," said the locksmith, plainly disappointed. "That is an art, too."

"Oh, yes. And yet there is something impressive about painting. What do you paint?"

"Mesas."

"Ah."

"From the desert."

"Of course."

"This is a very big place," he said, and waved himself out, seeming, by his last words, to dismiss her, and her art, as acceptable but effete, using too much money, and too little skill.

23

"Since we are trapped here, we might as well try to figure out what Len was doing," said Paul.

Lise's spirits had slowly sunk, and she now sat with folded arms, staring at the late-afternoon light filtering through the steady rain. "If you want. I'm not interested."

"It'll give us something to do. Since we can't very well go out and collect butterflies."

"Have you ever collected butterflies?" she asked, as if only half-aware of speaking.

"Yes."

"What was it like?"

"I enjoyed it, actually. I always enjoy gathering information. Using my brains."

"You didn't feel sorry for the butterflies?"

"Sometimes. But they are, after all, insects. And who knows what insects feel, if anything." Although, he remembered the sound the soft bodies made against the glass of the killing jar, a fine, high chime of a warning, or even a welcome, across thin air.

"How did you kill them?"

"I don't remember. It was just a high school assignment. I didn't get any personal pleasure from it."

She watched the rain.

"I think you're allowing yourself to sink into a very bad mood," said Paul. "A very weak mood. You were so cheerful. It's still a vacation. Think of it as cozy."

"You think of it as cozy. I don't like it."

"So you're going to sit around and mope. That does a lot of good."
Paul was worried about Lise. Her confidence was gone. As a result,
he tried to display more cheer than he could possibly feel.

"What would you like to do?"

"Like! It's not a matter of like. We're stuck. We might as well go
through Len's stuff. Listen to his tapes. Things like that."

She shrugged. "So, go ahead. Listen to his tapes."

Paul spilled the tape cassettes across the floor. They clattered
unpleasantly. He slipped the one closest to him into the battery-
operated tape recorder and pushed the play button.

Nothing.

He turned up the volume, until the tape hiss was loud.

Still, nothing.

Or almost nothing. The sounds of someone moving around from
room to room, casually, the creak and murmur of the floor. This
floor, the one Paul sat on. A cough. The hiss of a sheet of paper.

Silence.

Paul popped that cassette out, and clicked another into the machine. More silence, and then the peal of a spoon stirring coffee or
something similar in a cup. The tinkle of the spoon tapped several
times against the rim.

Paul snorted. Len had simply recorded himself on his way from
one room to another. He had recorded the equivalent of silence.
Domestic nothingness. A harmless activity, he supposed. But very
peculiar.

He punched the fast-forward button.

A voice. He stopped the tape and rewound it briefly.

"I used to think so, too." Len's voice, he thought. Nothing more
than that. A simple statement, made to the empty air. Paul understood that. He talked to himself sometimes, especially when he was
cooking.

"That is exactly the point."

Len's voice again. Thinking out loud. In this room by the sound
of it, the voice was very close.

"Exactly. I wanted that total transformation."

Paul jabbed the stop button. He fit another tape into the recorder and listened to more empty, or virtually empty, tape.

"He's talking to someone," said Lise from the doorway.

"No he's not. Thinking out loud."

"No, it's the way a person would speak to someone if you only heard one end of a telephone conversation."

Len's voice: "You must let me. I have no choice."

Empty tape, and then Len's voice again, "You are so perfect. Accept me, no matter how limited."

Paul stopped the tape. "A lovers' quarrel. Embarrassing to listen to."

"Why is there only one voice? There isn't a phone here."

"Maybe she—or he—is answering very softly."

He stabbed the rewind button, and turned up the volume. Len's voice thundered, "I have no choice."

And there was no answer.

Paul turned off the machine. "It doesn't make any sense."

He wandered the cabin while Lise listened to more tapes. He deliberately tried to ignore the sound of Len's voice. He found a can of pork and beans in the cupboard and cranked the can opener. The single cube of pork fat nestled at the top.

The beans kept the shape of the can, standing upright in the pan, a cylinder of congealed beans. He stirred them with a wooden spoon.

Lise appeared in the doorway. "It makes sense."

"How?"

"He's talking to someone."

"A ghost?"

He was trying to joke, but Lise was grim. "There is another voice on the tape. You can barely hear it, but it's another voice."

"Would you like some beans?"

"Come and hear it."

"Lise, you're getting yourself all worked up about nothing. Len was just crazy, wandering around the cabin recording his own voice, who knows why, and that's all there is to it."

"He was talking to someone."

"In his head, maybe."

"He was talking to someone and there is another voice on the tape. Why don't you come and hear it. Are you afraid?"

"I'm not afraid!" Paul was shocked at the fierceness of his voice. "No," he said more softly. "I'm not afraid. I just don't want you leaping to all kinds of wild conclusions."

"I won't leap to any wild conclusions," she said, controlling herself. "Just come in and listen to this tape."

Paul stirred the beans once, then turned off the fire. "I haven't eaten beans like these for a long time. Maybe they're good."

She was waiting beside the tape recorder. He sat, and she pushed the button. "I will, of course, require manipulation," whispered hoarsely, a voice like none other Paul had ever heard.

"Play it back."

They listened again.

"See? Another voice."

"A visitor," Paul suggested.

"I suppose."

Paul made a weak laugh. "So he had a visitor. Big deal."

"Why aren't there any voices saying 'Hello, how are you, very glad to drop by in the middle of nowhere to see you Len, how have you been'? How come no one says anything like that?"

Paul shrugged.

"How come all we have on the tape is a very strange voice saying 'I will, of course, require manipulation.'"

"Odd sex practices."

"It's not funny."

"It's funny! Some old guy dropped by and Len was doing something funny with him."

"I have a very deep feeling that something terrible is happening here."

"I didn't want you getting excited."

"I'm not excited."

"Well, I'm not either, so let's go eat some beans."

"This place is hideous. We aren't safe here."

"We're perfectly safe. Is the river going to rise and wash us away?"

"I'm not afraid of the river."

"Ghosts! You're afraid of ghosts."

"If you're so smart, you explain all of this."

"I can't. And I don't have to. An assortment of random data doesn't have to be explained."

"I'm getting out of here."

"You'll drown." She was shivering, and he held her. "We're all right. I don't know what Len was doing, but I can't imagine how it could possibly hurt us."

"We could find a rope and tie it to a tree and one of us could make it across the river."

"Very doubtful. The current is very strong, and it's raining even harder now. And even if one of us—meaning me—made it across the river, then what? I'd be soaked, cold, and miles from anywhere."

"What do you propose?"

"I propose we calm down, and realize that Len was just a silly guy, totally harmless, who doesn't happen to be home."

Lise wandered to the metal box in the corner. She touched the padlock. "I want to open this box."

"Why?"

She looked at him, hard. "I want to know what's inside it."

"We can't go breaking open boxes just because we're curious. This isn't our home."

"We don't have to break it open." She fumbled through her purse, and brought forth a key. A tag dangled from it, and Paul touched it. *Dup.*

It looked, indeed, like it might be the key. It was the right size, the right weight.

He was very cold.

"We can't ransack the place," he said hoarsely. "It isn't right."

She looked at him steadily. "It's not a matter of ransacking. I want to know what is inside the box."

"Love letters. Legal documents. A pornography collection. A stamp collection. Drugs."

"Open it."

Paul could not move. The key was between his fingers, a neutral slip of metal, neither warm nor cool. It clicked into the slot in the padlock, and the padlock fell open.

"There," said Paul.

Neither of them moved.

The padlock glittered in his fingers, and he placed it carefully beside the tape recorder. It gleamed there in the early evening, reflecting the light from the ceiling.

The box opened, disclosing a row of manila folders, the tabs of which were slightly frayed. In the very front of the box, lying against the folders, was a cold tool the size of a butter knife.

"A scalpel!" breathed Lise.

Paul put that down, too, next to the tape recorder. He selected the first folder and leafed through it, with some relief. "Why, these are just pictures. More graveyard photographs. This is a series of the same crypt. Lewis."

He stopped.

"Let me see."

He gave her the folder, and his hand hesitated before touching the next. It withdrew the next folder, which left the box with a noise like a quick intake of breath.

Glossy black-and-whites, as before. First a sealed casket, shiny, like the husk of a huge insect. Then, to Paul's horror, the casket was open, to disclose a blackened, decay-splotched body in a suit. Picture after picture, some so close the mildew on the wing collar was plain, a spray of fine black paint.

The head had withered, and the nose had been eaten away, but the serene brow and near-smile were that of a relative Paul had seen in more lifelike photographs, Aunt Mary's father, the hunter, the sportsman brought down in a shooting accident.

"Don't look," said Paul, giving her the folders.

She looked, sinking to her knees.

"His grandfather," Paul began.

"I had always imagined," said Lise weakly, "that such bodies were in a better state of preservation."

"Colma is a very damp place," said Paul.

"Apparently so."

"Damp all year round, really." Paul had a memory he did not want to mention: the body he had seen exhumed, years before.

He put the folders back into the box, closed the box, and locked it. "So what?" he said at last. "We knew Len had a very strange hobby. He's taken up portraits. Portraits of the deceased. It's a harmless enough pastime."

"You forgot this."

The scalpel was icy in his fingers. It gleamed in the electric light, and he saw the reflected eye, his own eye, along its perfect blade.

"We are in the hands of an insane man," said Lise simply.

"I don't know about insane, exactly."

"You have a lack of imagination."

"You have too much."

"I don't mean the ability to see things that don't exist. I mean the ability to see what is. The power to comprehend what is implied. That is what intelligence really is. You are pretending to be stupid."

"Len has a fascination with death. Not a surprise. He has a fixation on the corpse, such as it is, of his grandfather. A sort of ancestor worship. A lot of people have a morbid streak."

"I'm leaving. I'm not spending another night in this place."

"All right. Supposing, just for a moment, that Len is utterly mad. He's not here. He's gone. We are all alone here."

The light from the ceiling dimmed, stuttered bright again, and then died.

The entire house was dark.

24

Sounds seemed suddenly louder. The pounding of his own heart, the heavy rain against the window. He began to see as his eyes drank in the dim evening light, and he felt his way to the wall switch.

He snapped it on and off, idly. "Well," he said, rubbing his hands together. "Lines are always going down during these storms. We have the fireplace, and I think I saw a flashlight in one of the kitchen drawers."

"I'm not spending the night here."

"You're going to swim the flood? You'll drown."

"I'll sleep in the car."

"No."

"It's better than in here."

"I don't think so."

"Why not?"

"I don't think it's safe."

"Not safe?"

"The bank might collapse. Get eaten away. And wash the car away."

"I'll move the car to high ground. What's the matter? You agree with me, don't you? You see that we're in trouble."

He studied what he could see of her face, a pale oblong across the room. "It's a little Volkswagen. It just doesn't seem strong enough."

"For what?"

Paul did not speak for a while. He found a chair and sat slowly.

"I don't think we should panic. We should behave like rational people. Sleeping in the car is a stupid thing to do. It's too much an admission of terror." He made a short, joyless laugh.

"I admit it. I'm terrified."

"We have to act as a team. We can't disagree with each other."

"Then we have to agree on what it is we face here."

Paul stepped carefully into the living room and knelt at the fireplace. A box of matches rattled in his hand, and he wadded a sheet of newspaper. "I don't think Len has lived in this cabin for maybe a week. Or two. Or even longer."

"But he left his camera. His toothbrush."

"We'll argue forever. We don't know. We are ignorant. His whereabouts are unknown. Some people shiver when they hear the word *unknown*. You could call a scary book *The Unknown* and people would be terrified just of the title."

A wooden match struck with a spurt of fine, white sparks, and a flame danced. Paul touched it to the crumpled paper, and the fire spread like black ink across the newsprint. Lise sighed and sat beside him, watching the fire.

"We'll be all right," Paul said, beginning to believe it himself. "Len is weird. We have no reason to believe he's dangerous."

"I know he is," she said softly.

Paul knew it too. The dream told him that. He had never paid any attention to his dreams before, and had always felt that people who preoccupied themselves with dreams were foolish. But this one was different.

"There is something you should know," he said at last. "Something I haven't told you. About the nightmares that I've had. They are the same as the ones you have had. A house. Like this place. Dark, like this. Someone in the house, walking slowly through it, as a paralysis grips you and you can't move or even cry out."

She looked into the fire.

"Aunt Mary has had the same dream. I put it out of my mind. I thought it was a coincidence. Well, it was. But I thought it was a meaningless coincidence."

"I don't want to stay here."

He felt weary. He couldn't argue anymore. "All right. We'll sleep in the car. I think it's a crazy thing to do, but I can't argue."

"You knew about these dreams, but you didn't tell me."

"They seemed meaningless."

"What else do you know that you aren't telling me?"

"I know that if we leave this house he can come back into it."

"That doesn't matter. We can stay in the car for days."

"It's awfully small."

"We'll only spend the nights there. And it can't rain forever."

Paul rose. "All right. Here's your raincoat. We'll sleep in the car."

Before leaving the cabin he stood before the fire. It threw huge shadows around the room, and his own shadow was a dark, quaking giant that flowed across the floor. He knelt quickly and put his hand around the handle of the hatchet. It wrenched out of the block of wood with a squeak, and he examined it in the firelight.

The wedge-shaped head was battered, and the shaft of the handle had once been covered with red paint. Now, the blond grain of the wood was exposed. The hatchet was the sort of tool that accumulated punishment, belonging to no one, used for one, quick violent act, then cast aside until the next task.

Paul tucked the hatchet into his belt, and covered it with his raincoat, zipping the nylon jacket, so Lise would not see it.

She had found the flashlight in the kitchen. It threw a brown oblong across the wet redwood needles, and spears of rain glittered in its beam from moment to moment. Their breath made clouds.

The river clattered somewhere ahead of them, and a wet branch whipped Paul's face, soaking him. The flashlight beam illuminated a fungus erupting from the side of a redwood, pale and moist as bone.

Lise stopped.

Ahead of them, tire tracks gouged the mud like claw marks. Rain pocked the slash-shaped puddles that had formed in the tracks, water as brown as milk chocolate. The light from the flashlight expanded upward until rain fell in its beam, fine and impeccable as a shower of needles. Then the beam tightened to a circle at their feet.

One of them had to say it, although it was so obvious they could not breathe for a moment.

Paul stepped forward and crouched, touching the long sierra of mud along one edge of a tire track. He stood, and turned to face the dimming light of the flashlight. "It's gone."

25

For a long time rain dripped from the hoods of their rain jackets as they listened to the crash of water through the boulders. Then Paul took the flashlight, and tried to follow the tracks of the car as if it were a wounded beast.

The ground was rich with a carpet of rust-red redwood needles, and the tracks vanished as if the car had been lifted up into the air. Beads of water stood out on his hand, and long slashes of rain scissored in the beam of light.

"So someone is still here," said Lise.

"A car thief," offered Paul.

"And we go back to the cabin."

The one place he did not want to go. But they had no choice. To spend the night in the driving rain seemed not only pointless, but an admission of cowardice. Paul would not allow himself to be afraid.

He held a branch so she could pass. The cabin hunched before them, a smear of smoke flattening as it left the chimney. "He's in there," she breathed.

"We are a threat to him, too," said Paul, and he was shocked at the harshness of his voice. "Wherever he is, he doesn't know what we'll do."

"He knows," she said.

Paul snapped off the light. The rain made a high, plastic rattle on their jackets. "If we stay together, and stay calm, we are stronger than he is."

"He's insane," she said softly. "That gives him a certain animal advantage."

"We're going back into the house, and we will sit in front of the fire, and whatever happens we will take care of each other." It sounded brave, but neither of them moved.

Paul did, finally, running in a crouch, gripping the head of the hatchet so it would not dig into his belly. He felt his way along the house, and then fumbled for the flashlight.

In the dim light, the cut end of a wire gleamed.

Paul straightened, almost glad. The electricity had not been knocked out by the storm. Someone had severed the wire.

They paused at the front door, listening, and, as they expected, heard nothing but rain. They stepped inside, and the fire snapped a spark out into the room that turned into a black seed at their feet.

It was this second coming to the cabin, their second arrival, that made Paul certain that something evil was taking place. The way they looked up, into the ceiling, as if they could see into the rooms above, the way they stood dripping, unable to speak, made him understand that he was ready to fight for his life.

"We will behave as if we have never felt fear in our lives," Paul said, unzipping his jacket.

She saw the hatchet.

"We shouldn't expect too much of ourselves," she said.

"But now I'm angry."

She made a strange smile. "Perhaps it's the place that is evil."

"You can indulge whatever fantasies you like. I'm reheating the beans."

"Perhaps the place broke Len, the way it is breaking us."

Giving people the same nightmare, thought Paul, wrapping his hand around the black handle of the skillet.

He wanted the cabin to seem different now, even more menacing and untrustworthy. But here was Lise's paperback, a detective story acclaimed by newspapers in Baltimore and Denver. Here was the water they had trailed across the floor.

Here was the camera on the kitchen table.

26

There was nearly nothing left.

A residue. There was only the Voice, and yet I stayed away, wanting what little that was left, and also because even then with His strength in me I was afraid.

But I came at last. The camera around my neck, running through the dark as a dog might run. I flung myself over the gate, and the iron I carried rang against it, just once. The long cold iron, the crowbar.

You won't have to wait, I breathed. Not much longer.

And the ecstasy blossomed in me, His Voice. The long, powerful Yes breathed into me and through me.

I was cold. This was the night everything would change. I would have to think clearly, even though so close to the Voice I was trembling, and my breath came and went out of me in bursts.

Headlights. So suddenly, puncturing the dark.

A black silhouette crossed before the headlights, far off, and a distant gate clanked open. I huddled. Small, I thought.

Small and invisible.

A car's engine, and the scent of exhaust, just barely. The headlights grew, and then they stopped, and a terrible thing happened, something that slammed me hard into the dark grass.

Be still, breathed the Voice. And watch him. This man—how little he sees.

A beam of light played over the stone monuments. The ugly glare bent and straightened as it stroked the stony shapes.

Then the light fell, and formed an oblong pool. And the pool shifted along the ground, coming closer. The wobble of light was approaching, and there was nothing I could do.

You see, said the Voice. You see how they are? That is the world of the living. That is the world you and I will escape. Look at how unseeing he is. Unless the light finds something, he will spy nothing but black.

The light made a sharp hole in the dark, matched by a tear-shape of light on the ground. The footsteps crackled along the sidewalk, and the man—because it was a man, a human, unseeing—passed within an arm's length of where I had become shadow.

The man stopped. The light swung far, and then it swung very close, so bright that it seemed to make a sound. The man's breathing was loud.

Loud, and slow. The man smelled of cigarette smoke. And I surprised myself by feeling something I would never have anticipated.

This man, this unknown nightwatchman, this ordinary human, could save me. Even now. If I reached out my hand, or if I said something. Even a whisper. It would only take a whisper.

Don't betray me, whispered the Voice. It was more than a whisper. It was a current, and it swept me before it like the briefest scum.

We belong together.

Stay still.

The flashlight traveled through the dark, and the steps receded. The man's pace, and the slow swing of the pool of light from side to side, spoke of boredom. The man had no special reason to suspect that I was here. He made his way back to the headlights, and then there was only the dark.

There, said the Voice. You see how he is. A living man, an ordinary human.

He is not like us.

A thought flickered in me: I'm human, too.

The Voice swept me. Even when you were a boy I called to you. Even then I had faith in you. And at last you have come to me. How I love you, Len.

You have never forsaken me.

I wept. I was not worthy of His faith in me.

Come to me, Len. Don't hesitate another moment. You have made me wait too long.

But still I did not move. I wanted to be what I was, what I had been, for a few more heartbeats, even as I begged Him to forgive me. I was not worthy of such love.

Come.

I trembled.

Come now.

The camera was heavy at my chest. The crowbar was black ice. My fingers could not grip it.

Come, beloved.

I crawled through the darkness to where He was. To the iron fence that held Him, and the iron gate. I did not know why I wept. I shivered, and, gasping, I worked the heavy, cold crowbar into the gate, and it rang against the black spears. I wasn't strong enough. No one was strong enough.

And then I was.

The gate opened, but caught, and I used all his strength, and then something else, strength that was not mine. With a noise like a bell, the gate opened, and I stumbled inside.

Come quickly.

There was a door, a simple, metal door. There was a keyhole. It was nearly too dark to see, but I was not using my own eyes, now. I had the power of the finest lens, a power no human could have.

Quickly.

I battered the metal door. It was bright where the iron splintered the coat of paint and rust. I heard my body panting, even growling, with the effort. The door would not give.

The iron punctured it, and then punctured it again. The door buckled, and the crowbar, knowing exactly what to do, worked its teeth into the bend in the door, and the broken thing opened easily.

Don't wait. Hurry.

Even now, at this last moment, I remembered enough to hesitate. Something held me.

Hurry.

It was cold. The floor was slippery with algae and water. I

splashed, fumbling, and found the great bronze cold Secret. I fell over it, and wept. I was here.

At last I was here.

We will not be mere man. Men are nothing. We will be something supreme over death.

The iron, the bronze casket, the air were all cold, but I did not shiver. I found the smallest crack, where the Secret was sealed. I leaned against it, panting.

It was bolted.

You can do it. You have my strength in you. They are merest slugs of steel, not even threaded. Why are you hesitating?

The iron did its work. A black split appeared in the casket. A bolt lifted itself out of its socket, and chimed on the floor. Another joined it. These were not human arms. This was not human strength.

Over death.

Hurry.

Another bolt. Until all around the bronze hull there were empty holes where bolts had worked free. I collapsed against the wall. My arms were numb.

Now.

The iron clattered where I dropped it. I put both hands against the top half of the husk, and pushed. It did not move. I heaved against it, groaning.

It did not move. I pushed from all sides, straining. I slipped, and found new footing, but the lid did not move.

Until at last it squeaked. Just that—a squeal of heavy metal shifting just slightly. Another push, and the lid shifted completely, with a musical, grinding sound.

At last.

I trembled.

Don't be afraid.

The camera clicked. This was a good thing—to keep this forever. You know what to do now.

I let the camera fall to the extent of its loop around my neck. But I did not hesitate. I was empty, now. There was nothing left.

I bent over the casket, and leaned down into the dark Secret. And it was not a secret anymore. I saw what had called me all those years. All those boyhood years, and into manhood.

Kiss me.

I kissed the lipless mouth, and reached around the damp body to embrace it. And something breathed from the body into me, and ate through what was left of me, a fire consuming spiderwebs.

And I would never die.

27

Mary had never wanted children. Phil did, of course, but since when did what men want make any difference? "I am pregnant," she had said simply.

Phil, who was still a tanned, sophisticated figure in her eyes, had gaped for a moment. Looking back over the years, she had always wondered if there were not just a touch of fear in his expression.

But fathers-to-be are always fearful. As they should be.

"I'm delighted," he had stammered. "Delighted." And he no doubt was, delight being a much more well-mixed bag than is commonly understood.

He immediately poured himself a splash, and tossed it off, neat, as usual, and ran a hand through his hair. "I had been hoping," he said. "No use pretending. I had been hoping very much. It's such a pity your father didn't live to see it."

A pity that Phil, too, was fixated on the man he had never met, sensing his better even in his absence. But she had responded regally, "Not 'it,' dear."

And then the tedium of pregnancy, capped by the cesarean she was thankful for, since it spared her the dynamics of barnyard agony. The twinge in the side, the world-weariness, she could cope with. And all the while, nursing the delicate thing with spasmodic arms and legs ("Quite natural," said the nurse, reading her face) never dreaming what would happen to all of them.

Leonard had been Phil's idea. An unpleasant name, she had

thought, and yet dignified. She had never known where he had gotten the idea. Simply, "We'll call him Leonard."

And why not? Except that she slipped it into Len when he was only weeks old. Not Lenny, because cute names, like Jackie and Stevie, had always irritated her. Children were not toys.

There was an accident south of Saint Helena. A truckload of lumber was scattered across the road; it looked, when she walked up far enough to see it, as if someone surely must have been killed.

"No, ma'am," said the dimply highway patrolman. "Nobody hurt."

"How long will it be?"

"Can't say. You could double back, and cross over to the Silverado Trail. That'll get you on up to Calistoga."

"But I have an appointment in Saint Helena at one."

"I'm afraid you'll be late no matter how you cut it."

The lumber lay pink against the black asphalt of the highway. The metal bands that had held it had snapped, and snaked across the road.

She walked back, glancing at the cars she passed from under her umbrella. Strange how many people had places to go in weather like this. She was always surprised at how many people there were anyplace. When she got up early, four o'clock in order to catch an early plane somewhere, she was always surprised at how many people there were on the road, headlights blazing.

"What is it?" asked a pregnant young woman.

The truth seemed somehow too brutal to describe. "Lumber has fallen off a truck," she said simply.

"Can't they pick it up?"

"Of course they can pick it up," Mary said, irritated. "But it'll take time."

"Oh," said the young woman, as if she understood the concept of time for once in her life. "What are we supposed to do?"

"Wait, or else not wait."

"But I have to go to Calistoga."

Mary explained about doubling back to the Silverado Trail, but the young woman seemed disappointed in the nature of the world, and Mary wished she could explain something, almost an apology.

The young woman backed her small pickup out of the line of cars and drove away, driving fast. Mary felt her haste as a personal rebuke.

Mary sawed the Mercedes into the other lane, backed it around, and gunned it south. She drove fast. On the Silverado, going north, she passed the small pickup, its windshield wipers flailing against rain that was once again heavy.

Calistoga was a rain-stained clump of businesses and parked cars. Signs advertised mudbaths, and an old man flicked his cane at her as she breezed through a crosswalk.

From Calistoga she drove south again, by now resigned to the extra distance, the vineyards stretching to her left, long rows of plants with leaves as dark as meat. Water glistened between the rows of vines, and slopped onto the highway in places. Her car slashed through the water, and it gathered behind her, torn and healed within moments.

She found the realtor without difficulty, but sat in the car for a moment. His office was an unremarkable shed on spindly legs, obviously the sort of business she had always despised and pitied, the life's work of a petty person.

"I'm Ed Garfield," said the large, lumpy man. "What a shame it has to be such a lousy day."

As always with jovial small talk, Mary was both reassured and irritated. She set forth small talk of her own: weather, traffic delayed, surprise how many people have to be someplace, all the while seething.

She could not waste time.

She switched the subject, like a player turning over a card.

"Yes, a real nice young man," said Ed Garfield. "Came up here, oh, I don't know. The days kind of blur together."

"You gave him the key to the Parker cabin."

"I did."

"But you wanted to see me before you'd give me directions there."

"Well, I realize now that I meet you that you are a reliable lady. But the sudden interest in the Parker cabin. I don't know. It's hard to say, exactly. But it really got my curiosity, if you know what I mean."

"I don't."

"Well, it really got me wondering."

Mary controlled several kinds of irritation. She was not used to dealing with such cumbersome people, but she knew she could manage. She let her face relax, and lowered her eyes for a moment. "You do have responsibilities."

"Yes. My word yes. I can't just let any old body pop up to a property I'm in the position of managing. Of course, now that I meet you I see you're a reliable lady, so—"

"Tell me about the property."

"The Parker cabin?"

"Who owns it?"

"The Parker estate owns it."

"Who are they exactly?"

Ed Garfield leaned back in his chair, and regarded her with a look that seemed, for a moment, intelligent. "They are a bank, really. A trust for the Parker family."

"I want to know everything you can tell me. I am prepared to pay you as a consultant. For background information."

Ed waved a large hand, dismissing the idea of money, and yet the mention of payment had altered him, and he looked away, thoughtfully. "I hope there's no trouble."

"So do I."

He smiled, recognizing that she could be as laconic as he could. Still, he did not begin easily. His hands found each other, large fingers feeling large knuckles. "The Parker estate is one person, a sole woman. Elderly, now. And not what the courts would call competent."

"What's wrong with her?"

"She can't look after her own affairs."

"Why not?"

Ed Garfield got up slowly, as if in surrender. He slouched his way to a yellow coffeepot. "I guess you want the whole story."

Mary smiled. "Yes," she said sweetly.

"The entire saga of the Parker place."

"Please."

"My wife is not well," said Ed. "I look after her."

If this was an explanation of something, it left Mary mystified. "I'm sorry to hear it."

"You know how it is."

"Life can be unkind."

"But we bear up. Don't we?"

"If we can."

"Sure, we bear up. We don't have much choice."

More choices than we think, she thought darkly. But she smiled. "The Parker cabin."

He offered her coffee, and she accepted, recognizing that the ritual was a prelude, a setting forth of the props that would make him feel comfortable. When he had placed a bone-gray cup on his desk blotter, and leaned back in his chair, he said, simply, "Insane."

Mary waited.

"Estelle Parker her name is. Completely insane. Legally. And any other way. Sees things. Talks to things that aren't there. That sort of thing."

"Mad."

Ed grunted. "Altogether. Which is very sad."

Mary sighed in agreement.

"Except that the entire family has gone mad, one after another, some dead and buried up there, some being put away, generations of Parkers, insane, out of their minds, all seeing hallucinations."

They both listened to the rain for a while.

"You might say it runs in the family. These things do, I suppose. Genetics, that sort of thing. And then something very peculiar began to happen over the years." He gestured with a flat hand, slow waving motions, as if years were a series of gentle hills.

"Something very peculiar indeed. People who rented the cabin as a vacation place, weekend in the woods, that sort of thing." He prodded the side of his face with his forefinger. "They saw things, too. People walking around upstairs. Strangers coming down the stairs. People they didn't know. Unfriendly people."

"Was anyone hurt?"

"No," he said thoughtfully. "But scared so bad it hurts. The Parker cabin got the reputation as a place you just couldn't rent. It got a reputation locally, and generally I have had very little luck."

"You rented it to my son," she said, with an edge to her voice.

Ed held forth an open hand. "I told him all about it, and he said he'd heard about it. He wanted to stay in a place that was 'psychically interesting.' That's the way he put it."

Mary stared.

"He said he wasn't afraid. He said he was doing experiments. My responsibilities to him were clear. Ethically and under law, I have to warn him. My responsibilities to the bank are clear, too. Rent the place, if I can." He lifted the coffee cup, and then put it down without tasting the coffee, as if remembering that it was poison. "But I haven't felt right about it. Oh, when weeks went by and I didn't hear anything I figured, well I guess the Parker cabin is fit for human habitation after all."

"I want to go there."

"And then the other young man. Paul. Paul came here, and I told him to drop by the sheriff. Just to say howdy. Just in case. Because I had a funny feeling."

"I have to go there now."

Ed leaned forward, and put his elbows on the desk. "You can't. The road up there is washed out."

"You could have told me this on the phone," she spat.

"I wanted you to come up here. I wanted you to know what is going on here." Ed was crisp, suddenly. "If there's trouble, I want to help."

Mary was grateful, but confused. She had hoped that, at last, there might be nothing to worry about. "Do you think there is reason to worry? After all?"

"I called Al. The sheriff, an old football pal of mine, fishing buddy, all that sort of thing. Old friend. He said Paul didn't stop by at all. Not even for a second."

"So you think there's trouble?"

"This Paul seemed like a real likable fellow. He had someone with him, a girl, and well, I figured they could take care of themselves."

"I wish I could be reassured."

"There could be a lot of trouble," said Ed simply. "More trouble than you can imagine."

Mary told him, briefly, that she had not received a telephone call from Paul. And she told him that her son was disturbed. "A chronic condition," she said. Her worries about her son were compounded now by worries about her nephew.

Ed was thoughtful, pulling on his lower lip.

"But of course, there's probably no reason to worry," she smiled.

"A place like that calls to people like your son. It draws them." Ed's voice was quiet. He was almost talking to himself. "It draws people who are already disturbed, and it snaps them, like rotten lumber."

Mary was cold, and rubbed her hands together slowly.

Ed looked into her eyes, but did not seem to see her. "If it were any other place I would say don't worry. I'd say forget it. I'd say the phone lines are down, and there's no cause for panic." He looked away, and shook his head. "I should have warned both of them before I sent them out."

"Certainly you had no way of knowing—"

"I knew. I knew it as well as anyone. That cabin, that innocent-looking building in the middle of the woods, is an evil place."

Mary wanted to make a joke, something clever, but could think of nothing to say.

Ed gathered some papers, and thrust them into his desk. "I never had children," he said. "Not a one."

No regret, just a simple statement.

"Whenever I run across young fellows like Len or Paul, I feel like I want to help them, but I don't know how. I know a young man doesn't even like to be called 'son.' It rankles, you know."

Mary could barely think.

"It rankles their pride. And so I usually wind up doing nothing. No use going around trying to be a father to the world. I just keep to myself. Mind my own business."

"That's usually the best course," she managed.

"Oh, of course it is. That's exactly right. It is usually the best course of action to take. No course at all. Just let people go their own way. But this time. This time it's different. This time I feel like I sent two young men out into the worst possible situation."

He shut his desk with his knee and hitched his pants.

"This time I'm going to try and do something," he said. "I'm going to see what I can do to help you. Because if I don't—well, if I don't I may not be able to stand myself."

28

Ed's wife was a thin creature with red eyes. She crooned that it was a pleasure to meet Mrs. Lewis, and Mary sensed that this was the sort of woman who followed the society pages, and gave the invalid her best smile.

"We're going to be going out to look at some property, Sally. I don't know when we'll be back, but I called Tillie to come on over and look after you."

"Oh, it's such a storm out, though."

"That's all right." One of his hands covered both of hers. "Don't worry about a thing. We'll be perfectly all right, and it's not raining half as bad as it sounds."

Bric-a-brac. China birds nestled against each other. A woeful puppy. Handpainted pixies. Frightful junk, Mary thought, brushing by a chair with skirted legs. A Belgian carpet, and beyond, in the kitchen, a floor of green linoleum, split at one end, exposing a dark crack the shape of a knife.

"But she must have some coffee," said Sally, looking toward Mary and, Mary realized, not seeing her.

"We had some coffee in the office," said Ed.

"Oh, that stuff is pitiful," said Sally. "Just awful. I wouldn't offer that stuff to a snake." Sally looked in Mary's direction with a conspiratorial smile.

Mary said, in a tone that implied agreement, that her husband was very generous to offer anything at all.

"Oh, he's a good man," she crooned. "A good man," finding Ed's arm and patting it.

"What we need to do," said Ed, turning on the car heater, "is borrow one of those sheriff department jeeps. Four-wheel drive, built like tanks. We'll do what we can with that. Or, we could always borrow some horses." Ed grinned at the thought. "But there we're talking more man's work."

"I can ride."

"The main thing is we don't have to panic, or even work up a sweat getting up there. We just want to go on up there and check on them," said Ed, swerving to avoid a dead skunk in the road.

The skunk odor sharpened the air for several moments afterward, and when it faded Mary said, "We should hurry before it gets dark."

"It does get dark early when it's raining like this, especially this time of year. But I think we can make it all right."

For the first time in hours she felt a speck of hope.

"Unless," Ed added, "we can't make it at all."

The sheriff's department was a green stucco building. The lights inside it looked bright through the windows. Men in dark khaki rain slicks got in and out of pickup trucks.

"The place is a madhouse," said Ed, surveying the parking lot. "I've never seen so much activity."

He hoisted himself out of the car, and told her to wait. He'd be back in a moment with a plan that would work no matter what. Mary did not like waiting, and got out of the car and hurried through the rain.

Asphalt tile was splattered with water, and mud was tracked down the hall. A man with a star on his chest flattened a mop against the worst of the mess, but did not begin mopping immediately, as if reluctant to destroy a masterpiece.

Ed leaned against a counter. A woman with a pinched face and a microphone across her mouth shook her head.

Ed put both hands over his face, then turned and bumped into Mary. "It's a very bad situation," said Ed. He strode to a map on the wall. He touched it, and its plastic covering crackled. "The road out there has been covered by a landslide it'll take them a week to clear up. Not only that, there's minor flooding all up and down the highway beginning not five minutes from here."

"We can manage."

"Not only that, there aren't any jeeps at all. Not a single one. They are all over the county responding to this disaster and that disaster, and I don't know what all."

"We'll have to do it ourselves."

"I can't drive my Fairmont through floods and boulders and fallen trees. We'll have to completely rethink our plan."

"I'm not rethinking. I'm going out there, and I'm leaving now. You can take me back and let me drive my car if you don't want to come along."

"I'm not saying I'm giving up. I'm saying that we may have absolutely no way of actually getting there."

She ran through the rain, and waited for him to hunch his way to the car. He jingled the keys for a moment, and a drop of water ran from his nose onto his gray pants, where it spread and soaked into the cloth.

He started the car, but did not drive. "What'll we do if we do get there? If. And there is a problem. The two of us. What are we going to do?"

"What could someone else do that we couldn't?"

Ed drove. The car slowed to wallow through water, and for an instant the car floated as a spurt of water knifed under the door. The water curled in on itself and made a pool at Mary's feet. The engine coughed, and the car continued to run badly long after they had left the flood behind.

"Just don't want to see anybody get hurt," Ed said at last.

"Neither do I."

"Some of these sick people do some terrible things."

"Terrible things happen all the time," said Mary, growing very cold.

"Like Estelle. A nice lady. Quiet, from what people could see of her when she came down into town. About your size, and looked a little like you."

Vineyards unfolded in all directions, black and dark red vines, and yellow vines, with here and there a house behind dark trees.

"When she went mad she did something no one could have ever dreamed possible."

"What, exactly?"

"I really don't want to go into the details."

"Don't be ridiculous. I want to know everything."

"Well, basically—"

"Everything."

The road dipped and water arced on each side of the car. Water thundered beneath the floor of the car, and then the road curved over a rise, past a rusted truck on wooden blocks.

Mary opened her purse and found her compact.

Ed continued, "She broke an ice pick off in her sister's head, and when that didn't work she cut a big wedge out of her throat, like a piece of pie."

Mary's own eyes looked into themselves, trembling with the movement of the car.

"I had an interview with her after she did it. The courts still hadn't decided she was altogether insane. In so many words. And we had always been friendly. Nod to each other outside church, that sort of thing. So one afternoon I drove down to the hospital to say hello, and maybe touch on a little business.

"I was reluctant, to be honest. I felt real bad about her, but I didn't want to talk to an insane person who had cut meat pies out of her sister's throat. But I went. I am prone to fits of responsibility from time to time. Horrible habit. Drives my wife mad. I stuffed some papers into my briefcase, and I drove down to the state hospital. All the people down there know me. Lion's Club drives and all that sort of thing. So they said, sure, she's harmless, sit right down here and we'll have the little lady out here in a jiffy.

"She not only didn't recognize me, I didn't recognize her. She had a terrible grin, and walked hunched over like she thought someone was trying to tickle her. She sat across from me, and looked right at me, grinning. I opened my folder, and then closed it right up again. I talked the smallest talk you can imagine, and then nodded to the attendant.

"There was no use. She was gone. Polished off as surely as if she had died. Ever since then, I've avoided the Parker cabin. I have a caretaker goes up there now and then, but he doesn't like it. One tenant went up there to go fishing, and got so drunk he passed out and paralyzed his arm. Just like that. The house picks at you, like a dentist picking at your teeth, and if you've got a weakness, it'll find it."

"But you continue to rent the place."

"Life is complex. Maybe I should destroy it. But I have to think of it as a building that people can rent for a weekend, or a week in summer. Now, some people have gone up there and had a great time. Never noticed anything wrong about the place at all."

A place like that would destroy Len, she thought. She said, "What do you think would happen to you if you stayed there?"

Ed looked sideways at her. "You like to stir up trouble, don't you?"

"Well?"

"You're asking me to admit that I have a dark weakness."

"Doesn't everyone?"

"No, not everyone. Some people are solid. Oh, we're all human. But some of us are capable of withstanding all kinds of horrible pressures."

"I have always assumed that you could break anyone if you really tried."

"Well, that's a way of looking at it. I always thought you could withstand anything if you really tried. One of us would rather do the breaking, and one of us would rather survive."

Ed smiled, but Mary made a mental note: This was not a stupid man.

29

Ed asked her questions, which she parried, about her husband and where she lived. She explained that she was widowed and comfortable. At first she had the suspicion that Ed was interested in her in a bluntly sexual way, but then she recognized the garrulousness of a man who liked people and spent most of his time alone.

A dog-eared multiple listing book fluttered at her elbow and small calendars advertising North Coast Realty scattered across the dash. A business card bearing a blue-tinted photograph of a thinner Ed Garfield floated in water on the floor.

The car smelled of worn upholstery and the deep dust and oil scent that cars develop, as an attic develops the scent of mildew. A metal clip held a sheaf of notes in a scrawled hand, as if Ed had trouble remembering the small details of his life, and recalled all too vividly the larger ones, the families and the deaths.

"What, exactly, is the trouble your wife is suffering from?" she asked gently.

"Oh, a thousand things. A thousand things that might have killed a weaker woman a long time ago. But she's a fighter. A real fighter. I wish I had a fraction of her spirit."

Fenceposts held barbed wire up into the rain, and No Trespassing signs were punched with bullet holes. Even the speed limit sign was gouged with ragged tears, and the skull of an animal, elegant and pale, stared off across the road as they passed.

"Coyote," Ed said.

"I thought they should be larger, somehow."

"They're small, really. Small and quick." He said it as if sad, and when he turned off the road she thought that he had been overcome by a private grief.

They passed a sign: MCCORCKLE VINEYARDS. A gray horse watched them, and then turned away, up to his withers in gray grass. Ed stopped the car without any explanation and got out, squinting against the drops of rain that trickled down his face like sudden sweat.

He motioned her to follow, and she did, extricating her umbrella from the back seat. Ed's manners, she reflected, were a little shabby, but she could not manage to be offended.

A huge place, dark, and smelling of wine. Or of the wine process: a sweet decay everywhere. Her steps resounded off the concrete floor, and were lost in the quiet of the barrels.

"Ed," echoed a voice.

A young man put down a book, and Ed shook his hand and made a casual introduction. Complaints about the weather, the lack of business, and human frailty in general.

"I sent someone out to the old Parker place a few days ago."

"I know," said the young man, whose name was Randolph. "They stopped by and did some tasting. They bought some. Seemed pleased with it."

"Of course they were pleased with it. This is one of the very best. Bar none."

Randolph turned a page in his receipt book. "Two of our sauternes. I could tell he liked it from the moment he tasted it." He looked from one to another of them. "There's something wrong, isn't there?"

"That's what we want to know."

"I hate that place!" said Randolph with such vehemence his voice resonated in the darkness above them. "I wish the place would burn, except burning would probably cast the evil all over the valley."

Mary was stunned.

"Anyway, you won't be able to get in there," Randolph continued. "The road has never been much. More of a rough sketch than a road. There's a landslide right where it meets the highway. Mud and boulders and roots. There's no way."

"We can borrow your jeep," Ed replied.

"The jeep won't make it over those boulders." Randolph said this as if he didn't want it to.

"We can try," Ed snapped.

"I'll be glad to compensate you for the trouble," Mary said, twitching her purse.

Randolph laughed. "There are limits to what a jeep can do. It's not a helicopter. It's not a magic carpet. This thing is just a battered tin can. A four-wheel-drive tin can, okay, but it has big miles on it, and you just can't expect—"

He met their stares, and looked down.

"I'll snap an axle," he murmured, finally.

"I'll buy the jeep. Whatever you ask. Money is not an issue."

Randolph eyed her.

"So, you see," Ed said, clapping a hand on Randolph's shoulder. "You can't lose!"

Randolph tossed the receipt book to the desk. "I can always lose."

"No time for pessimism. This lady's worried about her son. You'll loan the jeep, and you'll drive it, too."

"The sheriff says it'll take them a week, and they might as well not bother. They started to push at it, but the crew gave up, or got called somewhere else. Just scraped it off the main road like so much sh—" Randolph stopped himself, and for a moment Mary thought that under very different circumstances she might be able to tolerate him.

"It'll be dark in another hour," Ed said quietly. "We might as well get started."

Randolph laughed. "Get started going nowhere." But he picked up a yellow slicker lying on the floor in a puddle of its own making. "Get started letting my jeep sink to the bottom of a mud pile."

"You go on and get the jeep," said Ed quietly, "and lock this place up, or whatever you have to do. We'll be waiting outside."

They stood under the edge of the roof. The horse watched them, as if he could not believe they were real. He put his head down to the grass, and then looked up again, glistening with water.

A sliding door groaned, and a lock rattled. Rain fell as far as she could see, until the hills across the road rose into the low clouds.

An engine rumbled, and a white jeep rolled around the corner of the building.

Except that it wasn't entirely white. Rust holes gaped along the bottom of the chassis, and red rust divots scarred the hood. Rust had wept from the sores in the paint, and the tires were gouged. There was no top, and already water pooled in the valleys in the seats.

Randolph grinned from under a yellow rain hat like an inverted dish. "You'll see what I mean. We'll be back in ten minutes."

Mary erected her umbrella, and sat in the back of the jeep, facing sideways. She gripped the umbrella hard, and lurched with the jeep as it bounded over ruts. She barely noticed where they were going.

She found that she had closed her eyes. When she opened them, fenceposts blurred past, and she had to fight her umbrella and finally close it. Rain ran through her hair like icy fingers, but she didn't mind it. She was going to be cleansed of all the bad things.

The jeep wrenched to a stop. "See!" cried Randolph. "There's no way."

The side of a mountain had collapsed, leaving a cliff-face like a sliced loaf. Gray-blue stones the size of human heads scattered across a pudding of smaller, more jagged stones, and black roots stitched the surface.

30

The deer head looked down upon them as they sat before the fire-place. Paul cradled the hatchet as if it were a delicate relic, and Lise stabbed another stick into the fire.

"In a way," Paul said, "I'm glad Len—or someone—hid the car."

Lise hefted the poker and glanced at him.

"It makes it a criminal matter," said Paul. "A matter for the police."

"And that pleases you?"

"It brings it into the light of common experience. We aren't afraid of an evil place, or an evil person. We are harassed by a thief."

"I find it difficult to be reassured." Lise tried to be calm, even flippant, but Paul knew that her preoccupation with the fire was too intense. She constantly poked it, shoving logs, sending a train of gilt sparks up the chimney. She could not sit still.

She wrestled another log over the hearth. She nudged the wood box with her foot. "I have some bad news."

Paul rose to help her.

"This is the last log," she said.

A few scraps of wood, like monkey droppings, scattered across the dark interior of the box. Paul kicked the box, and it thumped like a large, empty trunk. "There's a woodpile behind the cabin," he said. "I'll go get some more."

She clutched his arm. "You're not leaving me in here alone!"

Paul faked a laugh. "Then we'll both go."

"He'll come in while we're gone."

Paul laughed again, almost genuinely. "For all we know he's up-stairs right now."

Their shadows quaked across the room.

"So what difference does it make," Paul continued, "whether we get wood together or not. Stand here, holding the hatchet, or come with me—"

The ceiling groaned. They both looked upstairs, as if the ceiling were transparent and they could see through it into the rooms above.

"If he's up there," she said hoarsely, "let's find him before he finds us."

Paul pressed his thumb against the blade of the hatchet. It would be a vicious weapon. He realized that he had never actually picked up an object with the conscious determination to defend himself before tonight. He felt, suddenly, very weak.

"You see," she whispered. "We can't do anything. We can't even protect our fire."

A log settled with a sound like a foot crushing snow.

Lise's hands were sticky with sap, and smelled of pine. He kissed her fingers and said, "We'll protect it. We'll search the upstairs, and we'll find him if he's up there."

She looked away. "All right," she whispered.

"When I was a boy I was afraid all the time," said Paul. "Every closet had to be shut, and the curtain completely drawn, not open even a crack, before I could sleep. I was afraid something would peek in at me. What, I have no idea."

He was aware, suddenly, of all the blank, black windows.

"So what we are going to do is go up and make sure no one is in this cabin. And when we have determined that the population count is zero, we will consider all the closets shut, and all the curtains drawn, and we will go get some wood." He liked the confident sound of his voice, and so he added, "And that's all there is to it."

"We'll stand guard tonight. Neither of us will sleep." Her face was pale, and she looked, suddenly, too thin.

"Ridiculous. We'll both sleep in shifts."

"All right."

"So everything will be resolved, step by step," he said, standing on the bottom step, as if to illustrate his point. Except that the hatchet in his hand belied the confident ring in his voice, and he felt his way up the steps, feeling his legs grow heavier and heavier.

She joined him, the flashlight in her hand spilling a dim oblong of light on the bathroom door ahead of them. The doorknob was cold, and the door opened with a croak, but the faucet gleamed and the room was quiet.

Paul touched the toothbrush. "So," he said, eyeing the bristles. "This room is secure."

In Len's bedroom Paul took the flashlight from her hands, and knelt beside the bed. A single dust mouse rolled over once with his breath. A button winked in the dull light, the button off a shirt, Paul guessed, a plain, white button, the sort of button that was always falling off one's cuff when it was time to hurry.

Had Len been in a hurry? Was he afraid to see Paul and Lise?

A few clothes in the closet, clothes hangers glittering like fine bronze hooks. A belt curled in the corner of the closet, an object Paul had missed when he had peeked into the closet before. A plain black belt, with a row of holes for the buckle tongue. Only one hole had been used, the third, and it was distended into an oval.

"What is it?" Lise hissed.

"A belt."

"You were staring at it like it was a mystery."

"No mystery. I have two belts practically identical to this at home. It tells me simply that Len neither puts much weight on, nor takes much weight off. A constant fellow. Steady."

The belt made a loud snap when he dropped it, and the buckle dragged for an instant against the floor as a kink in the leather relaxed.

Paul knelt and hooked his finger into a slipper. He shook it, instinctively, perhaps to guard against scorpions, but it was empty. "A leather slipper," said Paul. Gold-yellow words gleamed: Moss Brothers, London.

The perfect contempt for cheapness expressed in this slipper was obvious. "Len is a simple fellow, but he enjoys a little quality." The slipper dropped with a slap beside its mate.

The doorknob down the hall twinkled, and neither of them

moved. This last room was the one that seemed coldest as they approached it, and when at last Paul stood before it he could barely move.

"Don't open it," Lise sobbed. "Please, Paul, I can't stand it."

He gripped the doorknob, and turned it.

The cot was set up against the wall. The single clothes hanger gleamed in the beam of the flashlight, its color faintly red, like Mars on a clear night Because it was the only object of any kind in the closet, Paul touched it.

It was icy. Plain metal, like any clothes hanger, twisted into a hook. "Ordinary," said Paul, kneeling.

"What is it?"

"I heard it grind under my foot, or felt it. A safety pin."

Paul opened it, and closed it, and when he tossed it into a dark corner of the room it made a fine, dry rattle, and then was silent.

They made sure all the doors were shut, regretting that they could not be locked, and then groped their way down the stairs. "That's what is so striking about Len," Paul said. "He's so ordinary. I mean, apart from his odd hobby."

Lise stood in the entrance to the room that held the tape recorder. Although cluttered with equipment and tape cassettes, this room was plainly empty.

"Apart from his odd hobby," she repeated, and they held each other, suddenly weary.

"He has sturdy clothes, but apart from his slippers, they aren't anything special. A few photography books. Nothing special. He even drinks Folger's and eats pork and beans. It's not that he has bad taste. It's like he has no taste at all."

"It doesn't matter to him."

"Exactly. He's not interested in clothes, or books, or food, or music, or booze, or anything as far as I can see. Aside from you-know-what."

"So that his ordinariness isn't especially reassuring."

She switched off the flashlight, and they stood, staring into the fire.

"A lot of people have strange habits," Paul said. The belt, and the nearly new slippers, had made Len seem likable. Good old Len,

Paul thought, sardonically. Just a little bit off in his spare-time activities. Just a little peculiar. "Strange habits," Paul repeated. He was trying to reassure himself. It was not working very well.

She roused herself as if out of a daze. "So what?"

"That's a dumb way to argue. You can say 'So what?' to the most brilliant statement in the world. So, maybe we should excuse Len his eccentricity."

"I am not disapproving, exactly," she said.

"John Donne was preoccupied with death, wasn't he?" Acknowledging that she was a Donne scholar, he added, "I mean, that's what I've heard."

"Death is a common theme in many poets. Most good ones."

"I mean, didn't he sleep in his coffin?"

"Oh, that."

"Well, yes. The celebrated Doctor Donne, or Dean Donne or whatever he was, took naps in his coffin. Now that's a little peculiar, and yet people didn't go shunning him like a leper, did they? We have our private obsessions, but we can be perfectly normal in other respects, right?"

"He didn't really, though. He had his portrait drawn in his coffin, in his shroud, to be precise." He was relieved to hear her slip into a pedagogical tone. "It's a charming picture of him, a little silly. A man with an Elizabethan moustache and a dim smile wrapped as if for burial, but looking not at all dead. His eyes closed, but as if for fun."

"Maybe it was fun."

"He did it because he wanted to see how he would look when he was dead. The idea of looking upon his own dead face fascinated him, because of the sheer impossibility of it. He was enchanted with paradox."

"Ah."

"Naturally, there was an odd—you might say neurotic—element to his makeup. But there was a witty element, too, and I haven't discerned any such aspect to your cousin's psyche."

"You haven't really met Len. He was always a nice little kid. I didn't see him all that much, Fourth of July picnic, maybe once or twice over Christmas. For some reason my mother wasn't overly fond of Aunt Mary, although she always seemed like a very nice lady to me. I used to wish my mother were more like her."

"'Death be not proud though some have called thee / Mighty and dreadful, for thou art not so,'" she recited softly, watching the fire.

"Well, he may have gotten that last part a little wrong," Paul joked, but he could not laugh, and put out his hand to Lise.

"What's wrong?" he asked.

"There's something I saw."

She stood and walked quickly to the dark room, and stood in the doorway, the flashlight shining into the interior. She snapped off the light and backed away from the doorway, and Paul stopped her.

She was rigid, and she stared ahead seeing nothing. "The tape recorder," she whispered.

He extricated the flashlight from her hands and stepped to the doorway. He did not turn on the flashlight for a moment, listening. Rain. Outside, and above them in the trees, wind. Nothing else.

He switched on the light, the shaft of the flashlight moist from his hands. The clutter of cassette tapes glittered in the patch of light, and in the center of the confusion the tape recorder was a series of dim points of light.

Paul stepped to the tape recorder, and when he saw what was wrong he could not kneel to examine it. His knees locked, and he could not even back away.

The tape recorder was running, the tape turning silently, and the *record* button was depressed. Paul put his hand out to the microphone and covered it, and it was like covering the gaze of a terrible eye.

31

He turned it off.

"I knew something was wrong when I was in here, but I couldn't figure out what."

"You must have bumped it when you looked in here."

"Don't you see," she said, gripping his arm. "Don't you see what is happening?"

He rewound the tape recorder. "I've given up trying to see what is happening. I have decided to concentrate on not behaving like a fool."

"That's exactly how you're behaving. Pretending like your cousin is a harmless eccentric, and that I turned on the tape recorder with my elbow when I was in here a few minutes ago."

"I was trying to be reassuring. I know there's something wrong. Besides, I don't like being afraid. It makes me stubborn."

"It makes me want to leave."

"I have to stay here. It's a matter of pride. Besides, we don't have much choice."

Lise's distant voice rose from the recorder. "Death be not proud, though some have called thee—" He punched the off button. "I wonder why he doesn't come out and see us."

"Because he doesn't want us to see him."

Paul looked at her sharply. "You think you have it all figured out."

"I'm afraid I do. And I'm beginning to think I'd rather spend the night in the rain than spend it in here."

"You'll get hypothermia, and die," Paul said without conviction.

It was dangerous for her here in the cabin, and it would be wrong to ask her to stay.

"I'll wear one of the nylon raincoats over a blanket, and climb an oak tree."

It was a plausible plan, Paul had to admit, even if it did smack of cowardice. "Go ahead," he said. "Go ahead and spend the night up a tree, I won't stop you." He added, with unfelt courage, "I think you're making a big deal out of nothing."

"He's watching us, Paul."

"I'm going to get some more wood, and then I'm going to at long last have some pork and beans, and then I'm going to spend a long and very toasty night."

She followed him with the flashlight to the firewood under the roof behind the cabin. The bark of the wood gleamed bright as copper in the light, but as he loaded his arms with as much as he could carry the flashlight surged brighter for a moment, then faded to a dim brown eye in the darkness.

The stump of a branch stabbed into Paul's ribs as he trotted back to the cabin. The flashlight still cast a pale circle of light, but it was a meager improvement over total darkness. "It's a miracle it has lasted this long," he gasped. "A couple of batteries like that, stuck into the bottom drawer for who knows how long. They leak all their power."

Logs rumbled across the hearth, and one of them rolled across the floor. Paul parried an invisible foe for a moment, using the poker like a rapier. "So," he said. "We're all set."

His mock bravado had the opposite of the desired effect. She shook a red blanket off the sofa, and folded it into a shawl.

"I've always been athletic," she said.

It was news to Paul.

"And I've always been independent," she continued. She looked into his eyes, telling him things he could not understand.

Paul nearly said "So what?" but he watched the shadows that deformed her face and waited for her to speak.

"We have two alternatives," she said at last. "You can have the hatchet, or I can. I think you should keep the poker. It is a heavy weapon, really, and you seem to have a natural affinity toward using it."

The hatchet had been honed to a bright edge by someone in the recent past. He held it toward her, the head in his hand. She wrapped her hand around it, and let the weight of it swing her arm down.

"Don't go," he whispered.

"I am speaking very simply, and very calmly. I think someone is listening to us, and if that person tries to climb the tree after me, I will chop off his fingers." Her eyes were bright. "And his hand. And his arm, so help me God."

"I will not give in to it. I have a right to be here," Paul began.

Lise smiled. "Of course you do. If I weren't such a coward, I would stay."

"I will, of course, escort you to your tree."

"You are very kind."

Paul grinned, and it hurt. He heaved a log into the fire and smacked it with the poker. Sparks belched out from the coals, and steam rose from the bark with a sigh.

"Although, there are those who might say that if you stay in this house tonight, you're crazy," she said, zipping the nylon.

Never in his life had Paul had so little to say. He opened the door for her, and walked, feeling numb and too small for his clothes. He wanted to ask her not to go. He wanted to tell her that he needed her.

He wanted to tell her that he was afraid, but he did not want to admit to himself exactly how afraid he really was.

She walked straight to the tree, and Paul knew that she had spied it perhaps hours ago, and had planned this moment. It was as big around as a man, and three branches snaked out from the trunk just above Paul's head. Paul gave Lise a leg up, and she shinnied further up the highest branch, until he could not see her in the darkness.

The dim, gray eye of the flashlight stared down at him. He patted the tree. He had to admit, to himself, that the tree looked safe. He stroked the tree, as if the tree could feel him, as if the trunk would begin to purr. For a moment the tree seemed to quiver, faintly, as if a creature were trapped inside it, as if the tree had been a human and had been transformed into a rooted thing.

And then Paul realized that it was only the struggle of Lise high up in the tree to go even higher that made the faint shivering of the oak. "Good luck," he called up to her.

"Don't go back," she called down in an even voice.

"I have to," said Paul.

He patted the tree again, and when he wished good luck, a second time, he said it as if to the tree itself: Protect her. Keep her safe.

Water pattered around him: Stay here, stay here, stay here.

Paul had dropped the poker as he helped Lise into the tree. Now he had trouble finding it, and when he did it was hairy with needles and oak leaves. He held it into the rain as he walked, knowing that water was not the best thing for iron. "I'll dry you off," he said, and wanted to laugh at his concern for a lifeless thing.

But his lips were stiff. He touched the front door, but could not push it open. When he did, he expected to see someone there.

There was no one. Firelight glistened off the floor. The firewood sprawled where he had dumped it. Water dripped off the rain jacket as he flung it over a chair.

He had to. He had to spend the night here. Proving something, but he did not know what. Did he want simply to be proud of himself? Did he not want to appear a coward in his own eyes?

Perhaps, he thought. Perhaps he simply wanted to stay warm. He thrust the poker into the fire, but from moment to moment he turned around to see if anyone stood on the stairs, watching.

His own shadow, and the shadow of the poker in his hand, danced on the floor, a slow, lumbering dancing, the celebration of an event without joy.

Lise was right. It was an evil place, and crazy as it was to spend the night in a tree in the rain, it made sense compared with standing rigid with a rod of wet iron in his hand, looking upward at the ceiling, unable to move.

Why didn't Len just pop out from wherever he was? If he was watching them, why didn't he show himself? What was he afraid of?

Afraid of being seen.

Paul could no longer rationalize what Len had done. He had tried to be cheerful. Now he had to be honest with himself. Len was more than shy. He was not simply a man who wanted to be alone. Besides, he wasn't a complete hermit. That man with the rasping whisper, that voice on the tape. That was a visitor, wasn't he?

But whatever Len was, he was sick. There was no question about that now. False cheer could not save Paul. The old, rational world had melted away.

Paul paced the floor, carrying the poker like a stick with which he was about to beat a dog. The shadow of the poker rose and fell against the wall, a misshapen club. Paul plucked a pinecone off the hearth, and tossed it into the fire. It hissed, and blazed with white flame.

He stabbed the poker into the fire, deep into the coals. People alone like this had to be careful. They could become so frightened, so terrified, that they might begin to imagine things. No doubt, he reasoned, that was what gave a haunted house its reputation. The house had a combination of ingredients, appearance, location, whatever, that awakened the imagination.

This simple, solid building of native stone and redwood was exactly such a place. It looked harmless, but it was not. He would simply have to be strong. He would have to combat whatever forces were here with his own common sense. He had always had a good, skeptical mind. That's why he was so successful as a restaurant critic. His mind had a hard edge to it.

A lot of people thought it was easy to be a restaurant critic, even fun. The sort of job it was ridiculous to be paid to do. But it wasn't easy. It required fairness, for one thing. And powers of description. And a willingness to sample new foods, even if they looked like something mummified.

The poker was a dull red where its head was buried in the coals. Paul banged the glowing poker on a log, and cut a black mark into a length of unburned wood. Then he broke open an incandescent log, and gray, transparent flames danced from its heart.

The floor overhead moaned. A low cry, so much like a voice he thought, for an instant, that it was someone speaking. It moaned again, like a word repeated so someone might understand what was being said. And another voicelike groan farther on across the ceiling, a procession, Paul realized, of footsteps. A door opened like air exhaled slowly, a nearly silent sigh of pleasure. A floorboard creaked, and whoever it was did not hurry, did not, for a moment, walk at all, but waited, listening.

There was nothing to hear. Rain, as always, a sound so constant that it was like silence. The snapping of the fire, and a whistle as the last resin in the pinecone ignited. The pinecone rolled, a living thing now completely consumed into a shape black and definite as the head of an ax. Paul stared into the fire, his back to the stairs, as though the fire were a source of strength.

Footsteps again, to the head of the stairs, and Paul's back was alive as if a powerful heat were applied to his skin, and the shirt he wore seemed to shift, trying to escape his body. His feet were anchored, and his thighs knotted hard. He could see nothing but the seething fire, and his breath stopped.

Steps descended the stairs, slowly, one step at a time, as if there were no hurry. As if there were plenty of time to do anything; the night was long and there would be other nights after this one. No one ever had to hurry again as long as they lived, because there was time enough for everything.

The steps reached the bottom of the stairs and Paul struggled to clear his mind of the fierce whiteness that filled it like silt. There is no one behind me, he thought. It is the terrible pressure of this house, the power of it gripping my skull and sucking my sanity out like a syringe.

He commanded himself to move. He commanded his feet to up-root themselves, and turn because there was, he knew, no one there. He was alone in this house, and there was no reason to be afraid.

But his legs did not move, and he froze into a column of ice as the steps crossed the floor and a hand fell on his shoulder.

32

The Thing crept beyond the trapezoid of light thrown by the window. Rain streamed down its arms, and what was left of its face.

The living were still here. They had come for Him. They wanted to take Him back to the place of the dead. He hated the living, and wanted to destroy them. They were everything He was not.

He had been listening to their stupid, birdlike voices. He had seen them pawing through the possessions that were not theirs. He had smelled them—they smelled of warmth. Food.

He would destroy everything about them. The chimney smoke was dragged down to the trees by the rain. So He would punish them, like so much smoke.

The air hissed through his nonface. He was afraid of them, too. He was not alive, as they were. What could a Thing do, but wait, and hide? He was good at waiting. The dead do nothing but wait.

He made a noise like a laugh, but it was not a laugh. At first He had thought they would leave. There was nothing for them here. This was a place for creatures that were not alive. These chattering, lively beasts strolled from room to room. He crept from window to window, listening, watching.

He climbed up the rusting pipe and crawled along the roof. He could easily work one of these windows loose, and slip inside. He was good at slipping, and hiding. He was made of shadow. He knew how shadow crawls, when no one is watching, like the approach of night.

He made His noise again, His snort of anguish. Why were they here? It was because they knew He was here. They wanted to take Him back to the bronze husk, and leave Him there in a cold stew that would last forever. He crept along the peak of the roof, the very spine, where the roof would bear His weight without a whisper. Rain streamed into the holes in His head that emitted breath.

He crouched behind the chimney. The stones were warm, and He could not hear their mindless voices. The living had nothing to say. What could they report to one another? They knew nothing.

The not-living knew. They were the creatures with secrets. He gnawed at his hand, angrily.

He climbed along the roof, and slipped down the pipe. He panted, listening.

He was good at waiting. And he had a plan. It was a trap. They wanted to be here. Now they could not leave. He would wait for them to separate, and then He would take them. It would not be an act of cruelty, although they deserved pain. It would perfect them.

Even now He heard their voices. Brittle, empty voices, worse than the bleating of the lowest animal. But He would wait. He had waited for many years. A night, or two, more was no time at all.

A wait like this is like turning into stone. The Thing turned to granite. There were no sounds. There was no rain. No world. Only the wait. Not even a single point of fire in His mind. Nothing.

Vacant. Cold.

And then: One of them was gone. Steps, the door shutting. The one that fled did not matter. What mattered was that He could return to the place He belonged to.

This would be easy. His hands would have to touch them, and that would be no pleasure. The living were so disgusting in their warmth, simmering, quick.

The thought of touching one was nauseating. The crawlspace under the house was a good hiding place. The trees all around were good hiding places. But this was not the time to hide.

He could almost love the living, if only they were not so greasy with ignorance.

It was better to be dead than to be alive, especially if you were dead like this, supreme, and with a new life, a life the living could not dream of, that would last forever.

He would forgive these living creatures, but not now. Now they needed to be cast down, broken like a potter's vessel. He would show them how mistaken they were, with their quick emptiness.

How foolish were the living, with their many words. How they violated the silence with their chirps, and soiled the air with their laughter. The living fouled the dark with their naked light.

He would destroy them.

33

Randolph shook his head, water dribbling off his yellow rain cap. The jeep leaped in one place, and gears clanked as the jeep lurched backward and edged to one side.

"I'll get out and push," called Ed, and Randolph nodded agreement.

Mary got out, too, gingerly avoiding a stone that pointed upward like a stone dagger. She watched from under the dome of her umbrella as Ed put his shoulder against the back of the jeep.

The rust eyes in the white jeep seemed to look back at her through the growing darkness. They stared, neither kind nor cruel, but indifferent to what happened to her or anyone she loved.

She wanted to stop whatever Len's life had become, and free him. She had a confused vision of what she hoped for: mental wards, she supposed, nurses in white dresses and white shoes, Len sitting in a lawn chair with a blanket over his lap watching squirrels. He would put on weight, and get a tan from sitting between trees with the sun on him, and he would learn to be human.

And she would learn to be human, too. She would confess everything to someone. Dr. Kirby, she supposed. A priest? She had never enjoyed religion, but perhaps a palsied clergyman with white hair, one of those withered heads that had heard everything. Could she ask herself to speak aloud what she had felt? It would take courage.

All the while she knew it was pointless. Len would never be the hearty father, bringing children by the hand across a sunny lawn.

It would never happen. No earnest wife, no house behind trees, no career. He would remain what she had made him: a ghoul.

The jeep bounced over a huddle of rocks. Ed waved her along, but as she watched Randolph began shifting gears, then he put on the brake with a jerk. He twisted the steering wheel, released the brake, and looked back at them, wide-eyed.

The jeep tilted slowly sideways, toward a creekbed white with flood. The muck the wheels sank into was breaking away, a long, lazy crack like a fissure that might wend across the surface of a pudding. A spray of pebbles spat from behind the rear wheels, but the jeep merely whined, and went nowhere.

Randolph climbed over the side of the jeep, his face twisted with anguish. He stepped back from the crack just as a root snapped with a gut-deep pop. Like a hand slowly tilting, the shelf of mud slid down, and the jeep rode with it, making no sound in the thunder of water from the creek.

The bottom of the jeep exposed itself, a rust-black assembly of axles and joints. The jeep leaned against a tree with jagged, bare limbs, and went no further.

Randolph, his feet sinking into mud, covered his face.

"It'll be all right," said Ed.

Randolph did not move.

"It'll be all right. It's not going anywhere, that tree will hold it."

Randolph pointed, water droplets forming on his outstretched hand. "Look at that tree. That tree is pathetic. It's a dead tree!"

"It's dead, but it's still strong," replied Ed. "You can't see a speck of rot on it."

"There's no way it can hold the jeep."

"You have to admit the tree has no rot on it, now don't you?"

"Rot! The tree's a skeleton. It's all that's holding my jeep!"

"That tree has been there a long time, dead and alive. A tree like that has a root system as deep as it is tall. You couldn't topple that tree with a bulldozer."

Randolph held forth his hands in a gesture of surrender. He turned, but studied the ground, crushing a stone into the mud with his shoe. He shook his head. He would not meet Mary's eyes, but spoke to his shoes. "I have a feeling this is getting hopeless."

"There's nothing hopeless," said Ed.

Randolph shrugged.

"Look over there," called Ed.

Randolph looked after a long moment, but Mary watched the back of his head. Randolph scurried across the rocks, and climbed into a yellow bulldozer. "We can pull the jeep out!" he cried.

"We don't have a chain," called Ed. "Anyway, we're not here to rescue your car."

The vertical exhaust pipe vomited bronze smoke, the lid that covered it dancing up and down. Randolph worked levers and studied the dials before him.

"I'll buy you a jeep, a new one. I'll buy you three of them. Anything you want," gasped Mary, struggling up the tread of the machine. She nearly slipped, and Randolph held her arm. "I don't want a new jeep," he began, but his words had little force.

"It'll be all right," she said. "You won't regret any of this."

"Ha," he said, without humor.

"How much further up the road is the Parker place?" she asked.

Randolph shrugged. "A long way. The road's rotten at best. And I don't know about driving this. For one thing, it's against the law."

"Don't worry yourself about that for a single minute," Ed replied. "I'll take care of any ramifications completely."

Randolph shrugged again. "It's very difficult for me to believe anybody, with my jeep lying there next to a flood, kept up by a dead branch."

But he squeezed the release on the gear shift, and the engine rumbled, shaking them all. "You hang on to this side and I'll squeeze on over," Ed groaned. "Too bad they made it for just one person."

Mary clung to the back of the black, tattered seat, holding the umbrella over all of them, although it did very little good. The bulldozer was bright yellow except where mud lined its edges and corners. The glass over its jiggling needles was cracked, and the metal teeth of its tread gleamed through red earth.

The machine lurched with a clank. At first it seemed that they were rising slowly into the air. The stones beneath them dropped away as Randolph struggled with levers that seemed too small for such a machine, black rods with finger indentations that Randolph gripped with both hands.

They were not rising into the air, but clanking over a ridge of earth. They balanced over it, then fell forward, all of them gasping, then staggering as Randolph struggled around a boulder.

"Slow down!" cried Ed.

"I don't even know how to speed up," said Randolph thoughtfully. "This is a very strange piece of equipment."

A pale tree sprawled, half collapsed, before them. Randolph wrestled with the levers, then pressed a pedal with his foot, and leaned back as if to distance himself from what was about to happen. "Hang on," he said, nearly inaudible.

They drove up the tree, and then stopped. The machine tilted to one side, then corrected itself, and slumped over to the other. Mary gripped the back of the seat until it hurt, and then with a bang the tree broke, and the bulldozer skidded down a long slope scattered with blue rocks.

The metal tread clanked over the stones, mud jiggling along it like dirt delivered by a conveyor belt. The machine surged up a slope, coughing and bellowing.

"This is a very peculiar vehicle," said Randolph. "It handles in a very awkward way. You'd have to say it doesn't handle at all."

They swayed and jiggled over the edge of a bank, and the bulldozer clattered across meager asphalt. "The road," Ed called.

Mary gripped her umbrella. It was obviously a road, and it was obviously a very poor one. It caved away in some places, and water gushed across it in others. It was appalling that a road as badly maintained as this could be allowed to exist. Even where there was asphalt, there were holes eaten away, and the yellow underbed was exposed, stones packed together like discolored molars.

But what disturbed her most was the growing darkness. It gathered in culverts, where manzanita twisted against the wet earth. It filled the creekbed where boulders churned. It dissolved the road ahead of them.

"How much farther?" she called over the rumble of the engine.

"Quite a ways," Ed said, as the bulldozer careened up an embankment to avoid a hole scooped out of the side of the road. "I'm afraid it'll be dark by the time we get there, but that probably won't make a whole lot of difference."

A tree had fallen over the road, a huge pine with scales on its sides so that it resembled a gigantic snake. Randolph jerked the machine to a stop. "We can't give up now," Mary breathed.

Randolph glanced at her, tilting his head up to measure her expression, perhaps, or remember who she was. "I'm not giving up," he said, sounding bored. "It's not my machine. If we wreck this, you'll buy another one. But you better get off for a second."

She and Ed dismounted. They shrank to the side of a redwood as Randolph clattered toward the tree and went nowhere. He backed the machine, and gunned it forward. Its teeth tore at the wood, but the tree rolled, staying in one place. Shreds of wood sprayed across the road, and the air was ripe with diesel exhaust and resin.

With a bound, the bulldozer rocked over the tree, and ripped the pavement on the other side. Mary struggled back to the bulldozer, surprised at the hand Randolph gave her, gripping her hard just above her wrist.

Then the machine rumbled forward, the sound of its engine louder as the darkness increased.

For a moment Mary had the vision of the three of them seated around a fire. Paul telling stories of famous chefs, while Len listened, making bright, appropriate comments, and the woman, whoever she was, knitted, or leafed through a magazine. They would burst in on them, and there would be embarrassment and laughter, and they would all have rum and something, hot water and lemon, if nothing else, and share a long evening together.

Randolph fumbled with switches, and headlights speared the dark. Crumbled pavement rattled toward them in the twin beams, and the edges of the road were cluttered with the branches of redwoods and the featherlike fronds of ferns.

Len would have used his stay in the woods to strengthen himself. He would have been hiking, and chopping wood. He would still be a wraith, but a stronger one, and one with a future. He would be surprised and pleased at her visit, because surely he still cared for her, surely there was still affection between them.

The bulldozer shrieked. Its metal teeth ground along the pavement, slipping, then biting. The machine rocked forward, and the headlights revealed a chasm, fresh and naked, fragments of broken asphalt scattered across red dirt. A white knot of water struggled at the bottom.

"How much farther?" she asked when she could speak.

"I don't know," said Randolph.

"Hard to say, exactly," Ed mused. "Tell you the truth, I've lost track of where exactly we are."

"We are," said Randolph, "as far as we can go." He slung a foot up over the side of the machine, where rain pattered onto his pantleg. "We have here an uncrossable canyon."

Mary clawed down from the bulldozer, and stepped back from the dark cavern before them.

"It didn't used to be here, as far as I can remember," said Randolph.

"Where are you going?" Ed called.

Mary half-fell into the chasm, skidded down the mud, and struggled across the gush of water. Her umbrella collapsed, its wire ribs protruding from the cloth. She hurled the umbrella into the white water, as she clambered slowly up the other bank.

Mud filled her shoes, and her stringy hair half-blinded her as she wrestled up the opposite edge, and turned, blinking in the headlights.

She ran on, until the light of the headlights grew dim, and the cries of her companions diminished and were lost in the steady rain. She ran gasping, only guessing that she could reach the cabin, wherever it was, believing that the darkness that captured her was a good sign, a promising omen, proof that nightmares do not have to come true.

34

The river roiled in the darkness, and the thunder of it shook her. She sank to the ground, and could not move.

The rain felt its way into her clothes, but she did not shrink from it. Her body was numb as she stared at the grinding water. She could not cross this river. It was too powerful, too wide.

She was beaten.

She had been foolish. And yet—she knew her son was in danger, and she knew Paul was in danger, too. She knew something terrible was happening.

She climbed to her feet, and stepped to the edge of the water. She wrenched a branch from the ground, and tossed it into the water. It vanished at once, then reappeared in the dark river, the black arm of a swimmer who was already lost.

The forest beyond the river was a black wall. She could do nothing but stare at it, and at last she turned away.

She found the road again. She returned slowly, aware that each step took her away from Len. Rain stroked her cheeks like the unwanted sympathy of neighbors, and she stiffened herself against it. She would be silent in her defeat. No one would know what a chasm had opened inside her.

Two lights caught her. Twin smears of light gleamed on the patchy surface of the road. The rumble of an engine grew loud, and a hand reached down for her.

"You're all wet," said Ed.

"You made it," she gasped.

"It wasn't all that difficult when it came down to it," said Randolph.

"I take it the bridge is out," said Ed calmly.

Mary shivered.

"We'll have to take a look," Ed continued.

The bulldozer clattered forward, and when they reached the river none of them spoke for a while.

"That bridge was here for fifty years. Maybe longer. But there's no reason for it to go just because of that. Big old timbers can be as strong as big new ones." Ed pulled thoughtfully at his lower lip. "We've come this far like a bunch of fools. We might as well drive this thing across the river."

"That's a very dumb thing to do," said Randolph.

"That hasn't stopped us yet," Ed responded.

"We don't have any idea at all how deep that river is. Look at all that. The water'll swamp the engine, and we'll be stuck in the middle of nowhere."

"Won't happen," said Ed, gripping Randolph's shoulder. "You see that white water up there? It's not too deep, if you don't mind driving over a bunch of boulders."

Randolph jerked the machine with a clank, and gunned the engine. "It's a terrible thing to do," he said in a resigned voice. "We'll be stuck in the middle of nowhere."

The bulldozer chattered along the river bank, heaving to one side, and then another, as it surmounted white boulders. Randolph fought the machine into position, and the engine surged. "I've never done anything as stupid as this," he called.

The bulldozer rocked backward, eased forward, and the treads clattered across stones. The metallic chatter of the treads was joined by the rush of water. The steel teeth glistened, and the machine staggered deeper into the river.

It boiled around them. Icy water stung their feet, and the engine sputtered. The bulldozer eased sideways sickeningly with the force of the river. Its nose headed downriver, and Randolph struggled.

"You're doing fine," called Ed over the thunder of the river.

"We're doing terrible!" called Randolph.

Ed helped him pull the machine around, but they seemed to be making no progress across the river. Water streamed between their feet, and the engine vomited first a stream of black, then a stream of white as the machine stuttered.

The bulldozer fought its way over a submerged stone, and Randolph jerked gears, racing the engine, the machine going neither backward nor forward. "The middle of nowhere!" called Randolph.

They inched ahead, and once again the machine stumbled, and water shot between their legs. Water shivered off the gleaming treads, and they hung on tight as the bulldozer slipped and staggered toward the far bank.

A terrible force slammed them. Mary nearly fell, but hung on to the back of the seat. A black log nosed them, and ground against them until it forced its way past.

They were out of the water. The bulldozer threw mud behind it as they looked up into the rain. The machine fought the steep bank, but shimmied sideways.

"It's all right," cried Ed.

Randolph tensed, pushing the machine forward, but the bank was too steep, and they slipped sideways.

"We've made it. You can stop now."

Randolph did not seem to hear. The engine bellowed, and he crouched, fighting the bank.

"Let us off," cried Ed.

Randolph eased back in the seat. He looked up at Ed with a disgusted expression. "We almost made it."

"We're here. You did beautifully." Ed slapped his shoulder.

Randolph sat at the controls of the machine, staring into the rain. "We almost made it."

Ed took Mary's arm and pulled her up the bank. "There," he puffed. "That wasn't so bad."

"How far is it?"

"Not far," Ed said, fighting a branch out of their path. "Leave him," he said to her unspoken question. "He's developed an attachment."

Mary slipped on the roots of a tree, but kept herself from falling by grabbing the festoons of redwood branches that hung all around them. "Surely there's a path," she muttered.

"Of course there's a path. I'll let you know as soon as I find it. And I'll tell you what else. When we get to the cabin, we'll have a nice long sit before a nice big fire."

"Yes, we will."

"And we'll have something nice and hot to drink."

"That sounds wonderful."

"And we'll ask these people why the hell they can't call when they're supposed to."

But he was hurrying, in spite of the cheerfulness in his voice.

"You don't believe it, do you?" she murmured.

"Sure I do. I think we've just been overexerting ourselves out on the river a little bit, putting out just a little more concern than the situation absolutely calls for."

But he was nearly running, now, gasping as he spoke. "We've just been overreacting to your very normal concerns." He stumbled, but caught himself. "And once we got committed to a course of action, we were just too stubborn to chuck it and say forget this."

She hurried after him, because if she lost sight of him she knew she could never find him again in the darkness.

"We're just overreacting to the reputation of the place," Ed gasped, "and we just got carried away, what with the bulldozer and our own natural determination to—"

He stopped.

"What is it?"

"I thought I heard something," he whispered.

"I can't hear anything."

They were both trembling, and Ed gripped her arm. "Listen!"

Again and again through the hiss of the rain: the distant sound of a whistle, or of metal twisted out of shape in a pair of tongs. Or of an animal of some kind, an urgent cry, again and again, tirelessly, the shriek of a horse or a cat, a brilliant spear of sound thrown repeatedly through the darkness.

A human scream.

35

The steps crossed the room and the hand gripped Paul's shoulder, and he could not turn.

He knew this was not happening. Something about the cabin had slipped into his soul, and he was losing reality. He twisted his mouth, struggling to laugh at the phantom hand that had him by the shoulder, and he fought to turn, but he could not.

He could not turn his head.

At last his head began to move, his entire body turning, muscles pulling themselves around, like a body cast in lead. His eyes left the fire. Shadows quaked in the room. Rain sputtered at the window.

His tongue was stone.

A disintegrated corpse stood before him, its teeth naked in a lipless grin.

Paul put out his arms, but they traveled so slowly he knew they would never reach the thing that stood before him, its nose decayed into twin holes.

With a clatter the poker glittered on the floor.

The thing stooped to pick it up.

The movement changed something in Paul, and he could breathe. "Whatever you are, you aren't real," he whispered. "Nothing like you could walk."

The poker whistled through the air, and Paul staggered out of its way, slipping on the floor. The poker rose high into the air, and punched a jagged hole in the hardwood where his head cringed out of the way.

"This isn't happening!" said Paul.

The thing swung the poker straight down with both hands, and Paul lifted a shoulder. The blow stunned him, and he reeled to his feet in agony. "This isn't happening!" he wept. "You aren't real!"

The corpse before him lurched back for a moment, getting a new grip on the iron. Firelight glittered off its skull-grin. The twin caverns of its nose hissed.

Out of fury with the impossibility more than anything he lifted the only arm that still had strength, and blocked the poker as it whipped through the air. His hand seemed to shatter, but he stabbed his elbow into the grinning head.

The face slipped off his arm and the poker slammed his ribs. Paul fumbled for the poker with his lifeless arms, but the thing stabbed the heavy iron into Paul's stomach.

Paul staggered, and butted the thing with his head. The thing was shaken, and Paul groped for the poker with arms that trembled and jerked.

And then, like a sound seeking him from far away, he heard the simple noise of an iron rod colliding with skull. Three distinct white lights flashed to his right, and he sat slowly. He had no arms, and no legs. There were no sounds, and he tasted salt water.

There was an ocean. There was a wind, and choppy waves. There was only water. No sky.

He swallowed the warm sea. It made him feel quiet to drink it, and the surface of the sea stretched into a calm, perfect sheet of plastic. He blinked. There were lines in it. Parallel lines, pleasing to look at, and also tiring. He was going to have to count them.

Something sharp. Something jabbing, again and again. It was familiar, and he knew what it was. He rolled and a fire crackled around the black grenade of a pinecone. He lurched with nausea, and knew that the repeated jabbing was the sound of a scream.

A scream repeated over, and over.

"Lise!" Paul was on his feet.

The thing crouched, and Lise stood in the doorway, her lips apart like someone laughing. She screamed, and the poker rang against the hatchet in her hands, knocking it to the floor. She put out her hands, and grappled with the poker, but the dead thing was too strong. It wrestled her to her knees. It held her upright to steady her. It stepped back.

It planted its feet, and wrung the poker back.

Paul stepped slowly to the hatchet. It lay on the hardwood floor, like a thing that had been there a long time, tarnished with disuse. The handle leapt into Paul's hand, warm from Lise's touch.

With one fluid motion, Paul wrapped his broken hand around the handle, smiled against the pain, lifted the hatchet, and buried it in the shoulder of the standing corpse.

The thing collapsed.

Lise rose from her knees and reached for Paul. They held each other. Paul's arms trembled and he sat down heavily. "I thought you were dead," she said. "Paul," she wept, "I thought he had killed you."

Paul nodded, speechless. They both looked at the huddled thing in the doorway.

"I'm so glad you're alive!" Lise breathed.

Paul's tongue searched a gash in his lip where his teeth had bit into his own flesh. When he felt that he could move again, he crept to the figure in the doorway, and then froze.

The thing stirred. It moved its legs and lifted its head, and a thin hand reached back and tugged the hatchet free with a sound like a foot being pulled out of mud. The wedge-shaped hole filled with red, and a gout of crimson spilled down the back of its shirt.

The thing turned its ruined face toward them, and rose, hatchet in hand.

A large, pale hand closed around the hatchet, and a gentle voice said, "It's all right, Len. It's all over. These people are your friends."

Ed Garfield embraced the terrible figure. "Christ," he said. "Look what you've done to yourself."

36

Paul shivered under blankets, holding himself as still as possible so that his arms might not stab him with that white agony. Hours may have passed. He couldn't tell.

"I couldn't stay up in that tree," Lise said. His head was in her lap, and she looked down at him, desperate to keep him exactly where he was. "I kept thinking about this house. And how I belonged with you. And how wrong I was to let you stay in here alone."

"It's all right," he said. His voice was strong, and he realized that he would be all right as long as, no matter what, he never moved again.

"Because I belong with you, Paul. There's no question about that now."

"Of course you do," he said, before he realized what she was saying. "You actually realize that you belong with me."

"That's what I said."

"That's what you said. But if you extrapolate from that statement—Oh, Jesus!"

"What's wrong?"

"Nothing. I moved my finger. I was trying to make a point and I moved my finger."

"Don't talk with your hands."

"No, I won't. I'll talk with my mouth."

"Hold yourself perfectly still."

"I can move my legs. It's just my arms—Oh, Jesus!" In mentioning his arms he had gestured with one, and he waited for the agony to subside. "But if you extend that statement of yours to its logical conclusion, then you have to realize what that means."

"I know what it means. It means I'll marry you."

Paul blinked. "You will?"

"Of course I will. Did you ever doubt it?"

"Yes. I mean, I had my doubts. But I still believed that we'd— that something would happen to—"

"Something did."

"I knew everything would be fine," said Paul.

"You're delirious. You're in shock."

"I know it. But I am trained in being coherent, and even under these circumstances I am lucid."

"You'll be all right," she said.

"If I don't die of shock, you mean."

"That's what I mean."

"I feel great. Just hold me like this."

"I will." Her voice changed, and she wept.

"It's going to be fine," he said. "Wait." Salt stung his lip. "You're getting tears on me. We're going to be fine." She nodded.

The door to the downstairs bedroom opened, and Ed Garfield stepped into the room.

He picked up the poker, and leaned it against the fireplace. He did not seem to realize that anyone was with him. When Paul spoke he did not respond.

"How are they?" Paul repeated.

He did not answer at once. "All I know is Randolph has set back on that bulldozer. He loves that machine. I think he'll want to keep it. We'll have more help than we can handle by dawn."

"Is she all right?" asked Paul.

Ed leaned. He sighed. "She's managing."

"Is he still calm?" asked Lise.

Ed stirred himself. "Calm? Yes, he's calm. Practically asleep. Not that it matters. I have him so tied up there's no way he could budge."

"How is she?" asked Paul.

Ed rubbed his eyes, and blinked them. "I told her not to bother even coming in here, that she didn't even want to see. Didn't I? Didn't you both hear me say that?"

"Yes," they answered.

"But she said she'd come all that way, and she was the only one who could calm him down."

"She was right," said Paul.

"No mother wants to see her son like that. She's managing, but I'm afraid it'll be too much for her."

The door clicked. Mary slipped into the firelight. "He's asleep," she whispered.

She sat beside Ed, shadows trembling across her features. At last she said, "At least everyone's still alive."

"That's right," Ed responded quickly. "Everyone is still very much alive."

"He was going to kill you," said Mary softly.

"I had that impression," said Paul.

"He's been living under the cabin and in the attic. He was terrified of you. He thought—" She faltered. "He thought you had come to bury him. He thought—he thought he was a dead man."

"Dead," Paul said, shivering.

Mary spoke carefully, in a low voice. "He wanted to resemble my father in every way."

"So he used the scalpel to transform himself," said Paul.

"I'm sorry I sent you here, both of you. I should have come here myself. I was—I was afraid."

"But everything's going to be all right, now," said Ed, rubbing his hands together. "This cabin got its hands on an already sick young man, and nearly destroyed him."

"He's exhausted," said Mary. "From fear, and exposure. And his—his face." She did not speak for a moment. "Oh Jesus, his face—"

Lise went to her. "It'll be all right."

"It can never be all right," said Mary.

"At least we're all alive."

"His face is infected. I don't see how he can ever be a human being."

Ed stood and paced the room, his shadow rising and falling on the wall. "The main thing is, as cut up and hacked up as he may be, he's alive. This house"—his fist struck a wall—"this cabin almost digested three fine young people. But we got here in time."

"It's not raining," said Paul.

There was only the sound of the river, the churn and hiss on both sides of the cabin. Lise opened the front door and looked out for a long time before she said, "The river's rising."

"But the rain has stopped!" gasped Paul, struggling to his feet. His arms were in slings torn from sheets, but once he was standing they did not hurt. Or so he told himself. They hurt, but he no longer felt queasy with agony.

Water glittered among the trees. The current surged around the redwoods, and through them. The smell of water rose into the cabin.

"Randolph won't make it," said Mary.

"Of course he will," said Ed.

"Paul, don't go out," cried Mary.

Paul crept through the darkness to the rising water. A crust of forest floor dissolved at his feet as the water ate it, and spun it away. The roar of grinding boulders filled the air.

"We can climb to the roof!" he called. Then, to himself, he laughed. They couldn't climb to the roof. He couldn't, certainly, and Len was in no condition to save himself. This was the way things would end, washed clean from the earth. He did not want to die. He would do everything possible to stay alive. But if he had to die in this river he had accomplished one thing, one precious thing in his life: He had won Lise.

He trudged through the mud, grunting with pain, and looked up at the silhouettes on the porch. "I don't know about you guys, but I'm not going to drown."

"What do you suggest?" asked Mary.

"We'll build a raft," said Paul.

"That's right!" boomed Ed. "We'll knock a raft together in no time."

"Stop it," spat Mary. "I can't stand any more optimism. Look at how fast the river's rising."

"It's already past the trees," said Lise.

"So we better work fast," said Ed. "We can't just stand around like this. What's the matter?"

The buttons on Ed's shirt glowed. The outline of the roof loomed above them. Trees stood black against brown water. "It's morning," said Paul.

"What difference does it make?" said Mary.

"Yes," said Lise. "You can see red over there."

"Randolph has probably made it back to his place by now," said Ed.

"It'll take hours for anyone to come all the way out even to his place, much less here," said Mary. "We can sit on the roof, I suppose. And hope."

"That's right," Ed said. "There's plenty of hope."

A tree groaned. A redwood tilted, paused, and, like a weary thing, lay down in the water. The churning water tossed its branches, and the tree rolled.

Paul smiled. Perhaps it was because he was in shock. Perhaps this was, in fact, courage. But he was not afraid. "It's all right, Lise," he said.

She forced a smile.

The river surged higher, arms of it working across the soil, floating redwood needles and bay leaves. Earth slumped in places and was swept away.

"I love you," Lise breathed into his ear. "Whatever happens, I love you."

"I'm going inside," said Mary. "At least Len and I can be together."

"I'll find a hammer," said Ed. "We're running out of time."

"There's one in there," said Paul. "But I don't remember seeing any nails. We could use nails already in boards. Straighten them out."

"Now you're talking," Ed grinned. But there was a thinness to his grin, and he remained on the porch for a moment, surveying the flood. "We'll knock together a raft that'll get us out of here."

Lise held Paul, but she did not cry. They did not have to speak. "It's coming up so fast," she said, finally.

Water slopped over the edge of the bottom step. The roar of water shook them as they stood, like the rumble of a huge engine.

And it was the rumble of an engine. Something steel and gigantic.

Something impossible. The water flattened. It lashed against itself, and their clothes whipped around them.

A helicopter hovered above the water, and figures plunged into the river, striding through it. Men waved their arms in greeting, hurrying through the surging flood.

"A road crew came back for the bulldozer," Ed cried into Paul's ear. "Damn near arrested Randolph, but he explained it all." Ed laughed. "I don't think he'll be able to keep the bulldozer, though. I bet he's real disappointed."

Water lashed the cabin far below them. As they watched, the porch sagged and collapsed. Then they could see no more, as the helicopter followed the chocolate smear of water up the valley.

"What's left after the flood's down I'll take care of myself."

Paul glanced at him questioningly.

"I'll destroy it," called Ed. "Level it to bedrock. No one will ever stay there again."

Mary held a figure huddled in a blanket. Paul settled against Lise. Her breath soothed his ear, as sunlight gleamed off the dark glasses of the deputy who crouched before them. "We'll have you guys in Saint Helena in no time," said the face behind the dark glasses. "You'll be patched up in a jiffy."

Paul wanted to answer that he felt fine, but he said nothing. He smiled, and knew that the smile must seem the result of delirium—or perhaps the deputy was certain that he had two madmen in the helicopter.

Paul didn't mind. Lise held him gently, and he could feel the rise and fall of her breath.

He could stay like this forever.

37

He said, "Begin at the beginning."

There were stiff white uniforms everywhere. White shoes. Everything too bright.

"What was so remarkable about your grandfather?"

My lips were stiff. They hurt. I shaped a word. "Special." He was special because He would not die. Because He loved me. "Because He was so strong," I said, with lips that were barely my own.

He had been so loving. He had waited so patiently. And then He took me easily, with a kiss.

There was too much light here, and I wanted to close my eyes. I knew that light would cure me. It was so silent, though, and sterile, falling heavily from the sky.

Tweezers plucked gauze away from my nose. Eyes studied, calculated. My face began to hurt again. It felt like it was growing huge. Cotton rubbed cold alcohol on my arm, and a needle stabbed.

I was scattered, like a bag of leaves. Dr. Kirby's voice was raking me in.

"You'll live a normal life," he said. "Like everyone else."

To be normal was to be weak. To have no Voice.

The loving Voice would never come to me again. I was alone.

"It will take a long time," said Dr. Kirby.

I knew what this meant: It might not work.

"There may be days when you seem to make no progress."

I could feel the tape. A nose. The lips were like healed burns. They were raking me together.

"But we have time," said Dr. Kirby.

When I learned to smile again, I would learn to say without speaking: This is impossible, but I know you are being kind.

One morning Dr. Kirby asked, "Would you like to have one of your cameras?"

To hold, I thought. Just to hold. I nodded.

"You know the therapist wants you to enunciate as much as possible."

"Yes."

But I did not mean that. I meant that a camera would remind me of the dark. I had always understood the dark, how with time and care the camera could magnify the barest illumination into noon. It would remind me of more than the dark.

It might bring back the Voice.

I sat in sun some afternoons, sitting under a magnolia tree.

One morning Dr. Kirby said, "I wonder if you would like to see your mother?"

"Yes."

"You don't have to, you know. It's up to you."

Because I had not meant yes. I had meant that to see her would remind me of the Voice. That I was afraid. But that I would risk it.

"You're still recovering from a great trauma," said Dr. Kirby. "We can take our time."

So Dr. Kirby knew how to wait, too. Perhaps all real power came from the power to wait.

"I want," I said, "to see her."

But she did not come. I knew why. I was not easy to look at. I understood. They were gathering me, but it was taking too long.

It was afternoon, under the warm sun. A magnolia tree spread over me, tangling the light. Water somewhere pattered on the lawn.

A blond nurse stepped across the lawn, trying to avoid the glistening place where it was wet. Green grass clippings clung to her white shoes—two of them on the side of one foot.

"Your mother is here to see you," she said.

The water on the lawn was a long, airy note. Like the Voice.

"You don't have to see her," she added. "She'll understand."

I looked away. If I wanted to have a future, it would have to begin.

It surprised me, sometimes, that the nurses here could not read my mind. My thoughts were so vivid I imagined easily that they could read them through my skin.

I took a slow, deep breath. I let it go. "I want to."

She looked smaller than I had remembered. She looked away from me, and then looked again. I stood and held her.

The attendant brought a chair, and the two of us sat in the sun. There was silence. I understood my mother. What was there to say?

Her hand slipped into her purse, and she said, "Dr. Kirby said you asked for this."

It was my oldest, a Leica M2. I was trembling as I unscrewed the brush-steel lens cover.

"I brought film, too," she said.

The colors around me pulsed for a moment. This was the world that I could possess, if I wanted it. I was afraid, then, and held the camera to my chest. If my future became precious to me, because it was so possible, perhaps the Voice would come back simply to take it away.

I closed my eyes. The sun was a blush behind the veins of my eyelids. I spoke as clearly as I could. "Thank you for bringing it."

"I wasn't sure which one . . ."

I tried to smile. If only I could stay like this. If only the empty places in me could fill, slowly, with light.

"You'll be fine," she said, as though she believed it.

If He leaves me alone.

38

A life is a simple thing, she thought: You live.

Mark was waiting at the car. His face brightened when he saw her, but then he took her in his arms. He plainly did not know to ask.

"He knows where he is," she said. "And who."

"That's a blessing."

A blessing. It had been a long time since Mary had believed in blessings.

"Dr. Kirby is very pleased. But you know doctors. Sometimes I think they like to see people very sick so they can cure them."

Mark held the door of the car open for her, but she did not want to get in yet. She wanted to stay here for a moment. Mark was such a healthy man. So solid. He could never imagine what it was really like to have a soul like hers.

But Mark seemed to read her mind. "Isn't hope one of the great virtues?"

"It can be foolish."

"Never be too busy to stop and sniff a clover," her mother had said. Mary had dismissed it as the sort of insipid wisdom her mother was always offering. But that frail woman had done just that, and watched sunsets over the heads of tennis players, and gathered leaves while Mary learned how to throw a knuckleball. A slim figure in white, stooping to watch something small, an insect or a mushroom, while Mary and her father sweated, tossing a football.

"I nearly thought it was a bad idea to bring him a camera. I thought it might bring it all back to him. And you know—I think it might."

"The doctor wouldn't have suggested—"

"You're one of those people who have faith. I'm not. I'm afraid my son may still be lost."

Mark looked around at the parking lot, and Mary had to look with him. A eucalyptus trembled in the sunlight. If her son never recovered, all this would be lost to him.

Mark put his arm around her. "Just," he said, "a little faith."

A jay landed on the rail of the back porch. Paul had been feeding him every morning, ever since they had moved into the new apartment. The jay had a cultivated taste for puff pastry over saltines, but generally he got pieces of whole wheat toast and seemed satisfied.

Paul put down the chapter on soufflés. "All right," he said through the open back door. "I'll get you some toast."

The cookbook was nearly finished, and Paul had just given Ham the last review he was going to do. Ham had said they would miss him, and that he was irreplaceable, but Paul was glad to be finished with the column. Three magazines were offering to run recipes from his cookbook, and Paul's only problem would be deciding which one to sign with.

Paul broke a piece of toast into fragments. "You'll hide most of this, just like you hid all the others." The bird watched, bright-eyed, and when Paul tossed a crust, soared through the air and caught it.

Paul offered Lise the rest of the toast. "See if my bird will catch it for you."

"Your bird?"

"Well, I trained it."

"It trained you."

"Perhaps."

"He won't catch it for me." The jay flapped to the porch rail and eyed her. It called, a metallic bray. "He doesn't like me."

"Of course he likes you."

"No. Look—he's looking at you."

"Throw the toast."

"I'll feel awful if he drops it."

Lise did this often—refused to do something she thought might be a bad omen, as though this rational woman believed in good luck, or bad.

Paul folded his arms.

She snapped off a piece of toast. "He won't catch it."

"Go ahead."

"I've never had any luck with animals."

"Try."

She tossed the fragment of whole wheat toast into the sunlight.

The slowly turning triangle grazed the branch of the ginkgo tree, and spun upward.

It was snatched by the dark beak of the jay, who disappeared into the tree and called, high above them, in the universal language of triumph.